"You are such a wee innocent!"

Heath's cynical words struck Rana like a whiplash. Then he continued, "Your mother should be taken to task for letting you loose on the world!"

Rana looked at him in fury. "Why don't you leave my mother out of it?"

"Because you're being dominated by her." Anger was in his voice. "You're even letting her push you into marrying someone you don't love."

Goaded beyond caution, she swung her free hand up to strike his cheek. Heath caught her wrist as he mockingly said, "Nice girls don't hit their escorts, Miss Liscombe. Hasn't your mother ever told you that?"

"You're insufferable!" she seethed. Yet she knew it was true—she must free herself from her mother. Heath might be just the man to help her do it!

OTHER
Harlequin Romances
by JAN MacLEAN

2210—TO BEGIN AGAIN
2287—BITTER HOMECOMING
2295—EARLY SUMMER

White Fire

by

JAN MacLEAN

Harlequin Books

TORONTO • LONDON • NEW YORK • AMSTERDAM
SYDNEY • HAMBURG • PARIS • STOCKHOLM

Original hardcover edition published in 1979
by Mills & Boon Limited

ISBN 0-373-02348-0

Harlequin edition published August 1980

Printed in U.S.A.

CHAPTER ONE

RANA left the car in the underground parking lot and walked quickly across the tarmac, her heels clicking on the concrete. The vast, low-ceilinged ramp was lit every few yards by electric lights set in stone pillars, and the air smelt of stale exhaust fumes, and other less definable odours. The walls seemed to be closing in on her; the grimy underground cavern suddenly epitomised to her the sense of being trapped and oppressed that had overcome her so often since her return home yesterday. She pressed the elevator button impatiently, shrugging her slim shoulders inside the smoothly fitting dove grey dress; an expensive dress of impeccable taste that nevertheless might have been considered too subdued for someone as young and undeniably beautiful as she.

Within a few minutes she was pushing open the glass door to her grandfather's office. 'Hello, Miss Liscombe,' his secretary greeted her pleasantly. 'Nice to see you back. Your grandfather shouldn't be more than a few minutes longer, he has someone in with him.'

Rana smiled her thanks and wandered over to the ceiling-high windows, pulling back the soft folds of curtaining to look out over the city: steel and brick, glass and concrete, the muted roar of traffic, the scurrying crowds ... Edmonton, the city where she had grown up, and to which she had now returned after a year in an exclusive women's college in Switzerland. She gave a faint shudder as she recalled the college's inexorable routines and subtle, yet never-ceasing chaperonage of almost every minute of the day. She should be glad to be home, she thought, back in Canada where she belonged. Why then this surge of restlessness, this painful sensation that real life was passing her by and that if somehow she didn't break free, it might be too late?

Behind her a door opened and she heard her grandfather's jocular tones mingling with a stranger's deep voice. 'Ah, there you are, Rana.'

For a moment Rana stood still, her slender figure silhouetted in the sunlight streaming through the long windows, its rays striking white fire in the gleaming coils of her pale ash-blonde hair. Since she had been a child there had always been a special bond between her and Eli Liscombe, and so now a smile warmed her perfect features, giving them a life and vitality that in repose they lacked. Not even noticing the visitor, she ran towards her grandfather and was enveloped in a fierce bear-hug, her cheek rubbing against the rough tweed of his jacket. He was only a little taller than she, and as they separated, his shrewd blue eyes gazed deep into her own, so like his in colour. 'Time you came home,' he said gruffly. 'You look peaked.'

She grimaced indignantly. 'That's a fine thing to tell me!'

'She does look peaked, doesn't she, Heath?' Eli enquired of the man patiently waiting behind them.

Startled, Rana glanced upwards, to find a pair of granite-grey eyes lazily surveying her from head to foot. 'For one thing, she looks far too prim and proper to be any relation of yours, Eli,' he drawled. 'And I guess I'd have to agree with you. She needs to get out in the fresh air . . . to run down a hillside of daisies, wade across a mountain stream, or ride through a pine forest . . .'

For a fleeting instant Rana was mesmerised, as much by the vibrant timbre of the stranger's voice as by the poetic images he evoked, images that spoke to her confused spirit of freedom and space. Then she caught in his face the gleam of barely suppressed laughter; he was laughing at her, this arrogant stranger! She tilted her chin, her eyes frosty with disdain.

'Now don't get your dander up, child,' Eli interposed. 'Heath isn't the kind of fellow to make you pretty, citified speeches——'

'That's obvious!' she retorted.

'—but he's the grandson of an old friend of mine, so you can at least be polite to him.' Ruefully aware of her unimpressed silence, Eli continued, 'Perhaps I should begin again ... if it's formality you want, Rana, you shall have it. Heath, I'd like you to meet my granddaughter Rana Liscombe. Rana, Heath Markland.'

Almost reluctantly, Rana held out her hand. He was a tall man, Heath Markland, lean of hip and broad of shoulder. His hair had been bleached by the sun to the warm gold of ripe grain, yet his eyes held all the turbulence of a prairie storm. His face was perhaps too wholly masculine and full of character to be considered strictly handsome, although his strongly carved features and firmly held mouth—too firmly held?—commanded instant attention. Now that the laughter had faded, there was not a hint of softness in his features; rather the eyes that met hers seemed to issue a deliberate challenge. And then his hand closed around hers. His fingers were firm and sure and warm, with the same hint of steel strength that she sensed in his face. Her own hand felt small and oddly defenceless in his.

Abruptly she became aware that the handclasp had lasted far longer than was necessary. She snatched her fingers away and said coolly, 'How do you do, Mr Markland?'

'The name's Heath. I've heard a lot about you, Rana, from your grandfather. It's—interesting to meet you. You're certainly not quite what I expected.'

The man was outrageous, she thought in swift irritation, biting her lip to prevent herself from asking just what he had expected.

Again that sardonic gleam of amusement relieved the sombre grey eyes, and she knew he was only too aware of her inner struggle. Summoning all her self-possession, she said sweetly, 'But how boring life would be if everyone turned out as we expected.'

He nodded slowly and said in a seeming *non sequitur*, 'That's what's wrong with you, it sticks out a mile. You're bored by your life—aren't you?'

She gasped at his effrontery. 'That's ridiculous! Of course I'm not,' she said vehemently, stifling the tiny chord of recognition that his words evoked within her. 'And anyway, who gave you the right to pass judgment on me? I'm a total stranger to you, Mr Markland, and if I have my way, I'll remain one.'

Eli cleared his throat and Rana jumped; she had quite forgotten her grandfather's presence. 'Well, as a matter of fact,' he said, raking his silver hair with thin fingers, 'I've taken the liberty of inviting Heath to your dinner party and dance this evening.'

'But——' Unhappily Rana fell silent, knowing only too well how her mother would react to a last minute, and unknown, guest disturbing all her carefully planned seating arrangements. And besides, although nothing had been said, Rana was convinced her mother was expecting tonight's welcome-home party to turn into an engagement party; Boyd had been quietly and persistently attentive since he had met Rana at the airport yesterday. The introduction of an apparently unattached and undoubtedly attractive male into her daughter's life was not part of Dorothea's plan.

'The prospect of seeing me again doesn't seem to please you particularly,' Heath said dryly.

She blushed in shame, for she was a well-mannered girl. 'I'm sorry,' she said stiffly, 'it's just that my mother——'

'I'll square it with Dorothea,' Eli announced calmly; of the entire household, he alone had never been intimidated by Rana's mother.

'In that case, I'm delighted to accept your invitation, Eli,' Heath said. 'And now I must be off. I have an appointment with the president of the trust company in fifteen minutes. I'll see you both tonight ... seven-thirty, wasn't it?' He paused, and briefly, disparagingly, his eyes raked the girl from head to toe. 'Your dress tonight—it isn't grey, is it?'

She blinked, and stuttered, 'N-no.'

'Good. It doesn't suit you. Jade green, sapphire blue, the red of rubies ... those are the shades you should wear. And go for a walk this afternoon. That wan and pale look was all well and good in the Victorian era, but this is the twentieth century.'

Angry colour stained her cheeks and her blue eyes darkened with temper, so that her quiet beauty was transformed into vivid, passionate life. She opened her mouth to deliver a crushing snub, but before she could say a word he remarked approvingly, 'That's better. And remember what I said—grey doesn't suit you.' With a mocking salute, he was gone.

Rana let out her pent-up breath in an explosive sigh. 'Well!' she exclaimed. 'I've never met anyone so rude before in my whole life! Just who does he think he is, that high-and-mighty Mr Heath Markland?'

'I'll tell you who he is,' Eli said casually, although a secret amusement was lurking at the corners of his mouth. 'He's one of the richest men in Alberta. Made a fortune in lumbering, and now he's into oil as well. He'll go far. He's no fool, Rana my dear.'

'He's obviously been so busy making money, he hasn't had time to acquire any of the social graces,' she said waspishly.

'You'll be a better judge of that after tonight, won't you?' Eli enquired wickedly.

And suddenly Rana's sense of humour came to her rescue. 'You're nothing but a born troublemaker, Grand-pa darling,' she laughed, 'and I'm so glad to see you again. I missed you.'

'I missed you too.' His penetrating old eyes rested on her. 'Is everything all right?'

She shifted restlessly. 'Of course ... what could

possibly be wrong?' she prevaricated. 'Now tell me what you've been up to in the last six months.'

It was over an hour later that Rana stepped out of the building into the spring sunshine. She and Eli had chatted with all their old camaraderie about her experiences in Switzerland, about his business concerns, and lastly about her father's health, concerning which Eli was worried. Rana herself had purposefully steered the conversation away from any mention of her own discontent, for she could not understand it herself, let alone explain it to anyone else, even as sympathetic a listener as Eli. And she had not known whether to be glad or sorry that Eli had not once mentioned Heath Markland's name.

Because her mother's world revolved around entertaining and being entertained, Rana had met a considerable number of carefully selected, eligible young men during the past two or three years, even though Boyd had always been considered her steady escort. But none of them affected her as had the chance meeting with Heath Markland. As she walked along the sidewalk, idly gazing into the shop windows, she found she could conjure up his face in her mind as clearly as if he were standing in front of her. What was so different about him? An intuition that he was a man who made his own rules? Who lived his life as he pleased? And that he would be ruthless enough to take what he wanted, when he wanted it? The conventions of society, family ties, the expectations of other people; none of these would confine Heath Markland's roving spirit; yet how could she have sensed so much about him from an encounter that had lasted barely ten minutes?

She sighed sharply, trying to push him out of her thoughts. And it was then that she saw the dress. She stood still, heedless of the pedestrians eddying around her. It was the sole garment displayed in the window of an exclusive women's shop, and was fashioned of chiffon over taffeta, the filmy fabric so deep and rich a blue as to appear almost navy. The lines were simple, yet utterly feminine; the low V-neckline would expose far more of herself than either her mother or Boyd was accustomed to seeing, she thought wryly. But Heath Markland—what would he think? Would he find her beautiful in such a dress? Suddenly, irrationally, she longed to buy it and wear it tonight, so that he could see her in it. Only thus could she erase that sardonic gleam of amusement from his eyes, an amusement that treated her as though she were a child.

She took a step forward, then halted indecisively. Her mother had already bought her a gown and had shown it to her last night: it was white, with a daintily frilled high neck and long, ruffled sleeves that came to her wrists. Last night she had seen nothing wrong with it, indeed had been touched by her mother's thoughtfulness. But now it seemed all wrong ... Slowly she turned away and began walking back towards the car park, knowing how impossible it would be to explain to her mother why she had wanted a different dress ...

'You look sweet, darling,' Dorothea Liscombe said to Rana, looking approvingly at their double reflection in the gilt-edged mirror. The soft lighting was kind to the older woman, blurring the faint frown lines in her forehead and softening the rather thin lips. She was a handsome woman in her early fifties, her tinted grey hair arranged in a severe style that bared her ears, glittering with diamonds; more stones flashed on her beautifully cared-for hands. Her eyes were a pale, washed-out blue, that saw only two kinds of people: those who were socially acceptable and those who were not.

Now she consulted the platinum face of her tiny watch. 'We're half an hour early—that's good. Yes, that dress suits you admirably, dear.'

'Thank you.' Rana forced a smile to her lips, as she doubtfully surveyed herself in the mirror. Drop earrings dangled from her earlobes, a string of perfectly matched pearls encircling her throat; her mother thought pearls were the only really suitable jewellery for a young girl. Dorothea herself had arranged Rana's hair in an elaborate cluster of ringlets and curls on the crown of her head, the rest of her hair strained back from her face, which was adorned with only the lightest touch of make-up. The dress, pristine white, was pretty enough, she supposed, and certainly fitted well, but contrived to make her look both younger and less sophisticated than her twenty years would warrant.

From downstairs came the clear chime of the doorbell. 'Oh, that will be Boyd,' Dorothea announced confidently. 'I told him to come a little early, so he'd have a chance to say hello to you before everyone else arrives.'

Rana's heart sank. She did not want a tête-à-tête with Boyd, who, she was almost sure, was going to ask her to marry him now that she was home for good. 'Aren't you coming down too?' she asked hopefully.

'No, dear, you go ahead. I'll be along in a few minutes.'

Surrendering to the inevitable, Rana left the room and gracefully descended the curving staircase, her long skirt swishing about her ankles. Having just handed his coat and silk scarf to Henson, the butler, Boyd was waiting for her in the foyer. He came forward to meet her, grasped both her hands in his, and planted a proprietorial kiss on her unresponsive lips. 'Rana dear, I've been looking forward to seeing you all day. And how charming you look!'

His pleasure was so genuine and unforced that Rana couldn't help smiling back, feeling an uprush of affection for him. Boyd had been a family friend for as long as she could remember, had mended her dolls and taught her how to ride a bike, had squired her to her first dance and given her her first kiss. Now twenty-nine, he was following in his father's footsteps by becoming a junior partner in the family law firm; as far as Rana knew he had never rebelled against this course of action, and she was sure his conventional good looks and pleasant manner would be assets to his career. He was of average height, immaculately groomed, with regular features and straight brown hair firmly combed to neatness. He liked his life to be as neat and orderly as his person, Rana knew; no untidy emotions for Boyd.

Yet even as she thought this, she noticed a subdued excitement about him as he led her into the sunroom, closing the door behind him; he had brought her a corsage of pale pink roses, and while he fastened it to her dress, his fingers were shaking slightly. She thanked him, panic stirring within her, and said quickly, 'I'd better check in the dining-room to see if everything's ready, Boyd. It must be nearly seven-thirty, isn't it?'

'It's only quarter past—don't rush away.'

Still hoping to fend him off, she asked with determined brightness, 'How are things going at work? Are you as busy as ever?'

Firmly he clasped her by the shoulders, and again she was conscious of the tension vibrating within him, as he began what was obviously a well-rehearsed speech. 'You and I have known each other a long time, darling; we've shared a lot of different experiences together. I always have felt that a sound knowledge of the other person is the only sure basis for marriage. As a lawyer I see too many of these whirlwind courtships and sudden marriages, that predictably enough end in the divorce court. That's not for me.' He warmed to his theme. 'You're a lovely-looking girl, Rana—that dress, by the way, is sweet on you, most becoming.'

That dreadful word 'sweet' again, Rana thought irrelevantly.

'You're well educated ... and that would be important, if I do decide eventually to go into politics. I'd need a wife who could understand some of the complexities of our society and who could comport herself well in the public eye. I have every confidence that you would fill that role to perfection.'

'Boyd——'

He swept on. 'You can't deny that a marriage between us would make your mother very happy; she's always looked on me as a prospective son-in-law, and I have to admit I've been delighted to be considered as such. Let's settle a date, darling, and turn this evening into a celebration party—for our future together as man and wife.'

Finally he had finished. For a moment Rana hesitated, not sure where to begin. Then she went straight to the heart of the matter. 'Boyd,' she said quietly, 'all that's well and good, but you've left out the most important thing of all. Love, Boyd . . . where does love fit in your scheme of things?'

He laughed in relief. 'I didn't know what you were going to come up with. Of course I love you, Rana. I thought it went without saying.'

'I don't think it can ever go without saying,' she replied soberly. Leaving his side, she walked to the marble fireplace, absently fondling one of her mother's Meissen figurines. The last part of this speech had struck home; her mother counted on her marrying Boyd, and indeed had probably arranged for his early arrival this evening, hoping that he would propose. Subconsciously she herself had always assumed that sooner or later she would marry him. She was shrewd enough to realise he was offering her a future many another girl would envy: unimpeachable family background and social standing, all the luxuries that money could buy, a life of culture and security . . . why then was she hesitating?

For a moment she rested her forehead on the cold stone and closed her eyes, remembering how the walls of the parking lot had seemed to crowd in on her. She had the same suffocating sensation now, of bars closing around her, caging her in. It all sounded so predictable and safe . . . and dull, she thought with a stiny stab of surprise. What she was being offered was a life like her mother's; but did she want her days to become a repetition of Dorothea's, an endless cycle of dinner dates and appearances at the symphony, of giving the right parties to the right people, of morning hair appointments and afternoon bridge games? Yet what else was there? She fumbled with these unfamiliar thoughts, beginning to realise that her childhood had been so circumscribed, and her years of adolescence and young adulthood so carefully sheltered and controlled, that she had never known the freedom of making her own choices, or the excitement of directing her own future.

But Heath Markland knew all about that, she thought with sudden clarity, the image of his big muscular body and arrogant head somehow serving to crystallise all her doubts. 'Boyd,' she began, 'I can't say "yes". Not now. I don't know what's been wrong with me since I came back from Switzerland, but I feel so restless and unsettled.' She smiled weakly. 'Maybe it's just a case of delayed spring fever. I can't even explain it to myself, let alone to you. All I know is that it wouldn't be fair for either of us for me to accept your proposal.' She ran out of words and glanced up at him appealingly.

'I don't understand you, Rana,' he said, his brow furrowed in puzzlement. 'Tell me exactly what's wrong. These vague hints, they don't mean anything.'

This was just what she couldn't do, but she made a valiant attempt. 'I feel trapped,' she said slowly. 'I think I need to be on my own for a while, perhaps get a job and live in my own apartment.'

'You know perfectly well your mother would never allow that.'

'I'm twenty years old, Boyd! I can't be treated as a child.'

He shook his head. 'You sound so discontented. It's not like you.'

'I don't even know what I'm like any more!' she exclaimed, willing him to understand, or at least accept, her own bewilderment.

But instead he said briskly, 'You're behaving very foolishly. You're probably tired from a combination of jet lag and the excitement of coming home, that's all. Why don't we set a date in July, I'll take you to Hawaii for our honeymoon.'

She tried to curb a growing impatience. 'Boyd, I've just finished explaining why I can't marry you. Truly I'm sorry, I don't want to hurt you—but marriage is a big step, and not one I can take until I'm absolutely certain.'

'You know perfectly well it's always been understood we'd marry once you were through with your schooling.'

'Please, Boyd,' she pleaded, 'try and understand. I'm not playing games with you, or being coy and feminine. I'm not sure enough about anything to agree to be your wife——'

He stepped swiftly over to the fireplace, detaching her cold fingers from the mantel and pulling her towards him with an uncharacteristic show of strength. Taken completely by surprise, she yielded to his embrace, and his mouth fastened itself on hers. With every fibre of her being she tried to respond, but all she could feel was an increasingly desperate need to free herself from the stifling pressure of his lips. She pushed her palms flat against his dinner jacket, wrenching her head away.

'Rana darling, and Boyd—oh dear, am I interrupting? Why, I do believe I hear wedding bells in the air!'

Predictably enough, it was Dorothea. Wishing she could sink into the carpet, Rana fought to regain her breath, but Boyd forestalled her. 'Unfortunately, no, Dorothea.' He bowed mockingly. 'You see before you that laughable figure, a rejected suitor.'

'Stop joking, Boyd!' Dorothea said sharply.

'He's not joking, Mother. I've told him I can't marry him right now——'

'Why ever not?'

'I—I'm not sure I love him.'

'Rana, it's time for this nonsense to end! Naturally you're going to marry Boyd.' She continued with heavy sarcasm, 'Or do you have someone else in mind?'

'No, of course not,' Rana protested, her voice trembling in spite of herself in the face of her mother's barely concealed anger.

'We'll discuss this later,' Dorothea promised grimly. 'In the meantime our guests are arriving. Kindly go and put some rouge on your cheeks, child, you look like a ghost.'

Glad of the chance to escape, Rana started for the door, but her footsteps slowed at her mother's next words. 'Boyd, I'm depending on you to help me this evening. Eli has insisted on bringing a complete stranger with him, some kind of lumberman from the backwoods ... perhaps you'd be good enough to entertain him for me. And for heaven's sake, keep him away from the Spurgeons, you know how they feel about the nouveau riche.'

Swallowing a somewhat hysterical giggle at this cavalier description of Heath Markland, Rana slipped out of the room and fled up the back stairs to her room. Hastily she scrubbed some rose-pink blusher on her paper-white cheeks and reapplied her lipstick. She discovered she was trembling with reaction. The thought of enduring an interminable evening of small talk and dancing, where she would be the centre of attention, produced an actual wave of physical sickness. She took several deep, steadying breaths, and holding tightly to her courage, went back downstairs, hesitating only momentarily before entering the lounge, which was echoing pleasantly with well-bred chatter and the clink of glasses.

'There you are at last, Rana,' Dorothea said gaily, as though the nasty little scene in the library had never occurred.

With a strained smile at her mother Rana took a glass of sherry from the silver tray Henson was offering her. Quite by chance she looked over to her left. With a jolt of her heart she met Heath Markland's intent gaze. She had found him handsome earlier in the day in a dark grey business suit; he now looked devastatingly attractive in a tailored black tuxedo and white dress shirt, his thick gold hair curling about his ears. Nor did he simply look handsome, she thought with swift perception; he was also completely at ease in this rather formidable gathering of the cream of the city's society.

Wide-eyed she stared at him, too tense to produce even the semblance of a greeting.

His grey eyes had no difficulty in penetrating her fragile defences. She was certain he knew how upset she was, and that something was badly wrong, although he could have no idea what. Keeping his gaze trained on her face, he raised his glass to her in a mute gesture of encouragement, and smiled at her, a singularly sweet smile that softened the harsh lines of his face and brought a prickle of tears to the back of her eyes.

'Rana dear, do pay attention!' her mother chided, an edge of exasperation in her voice. 'Come and talk with the Farquharsons, darling, they were skiing at Zermatt this winter, so you'll have lots in common.

Immeasurably heartened by Heath Markland's unspoken sympathy, Rana did as she was told. Shortly afterwards they all proceeded to the dining-room, where the long mahogany table gleamed with silver and crystal, further adorned by an exquisite centrepiece of hothouse roses flanked by massive candelabra. Dorothea had made some last-minute changes in the seating arrangements, for Boyd, Heath and Eli were all at the opposite end of the table from Rana. Her father pulled out her chair, and she said gratefully, 'Thanks, Dad.'

He winked at her, before giving his attention to the lady next to him, and she took the chance to observe him more closely than she had since her return. He had aged appreciably since Christmas; he had always been a handsome man, and there was no doubt that his prematurely grey hair, coupled with the brilliant blue eyes that his only daughter had inherited, still made a striking picture. But new lines creased his forehead, while his shoulders, once so straight, were stooped; there was about him an idefinable air of private worries borne for too long. What could be wrong? Rana wondered. Just then he turned to her, making some trivial remark about the hors d'oeuvres.

'Are you all right?' she asked bluntly, knowing as he hesitated over his reply that she had not imagined the bleakness in the blue eyes so like her own. 'And don't just say "yes, thank you", because I won't believe you,' she added.

'You sound like Eli,' he chuckled. Sobering, he went on, 'I've had some rather pressing business worries, Rana, but hopefully in the near future they'll be solved.'

'Does Mother know?'

'Of course not,' Richard said, sounding faintly shocked. 'I never discuss business matters with Dorothea.'

Because Dorothea isn't interested, Rana thought with sudden, bitter insight. She had always been dimly aware of her father's deeply felt but inarticulate love for his wife, that had caused him both to over-indulge her and to protect her from reality; he belonged to the old school, that believed in sheltering their womenfolk. On the other side of the coin, Dorothea was content to have it so; as long as she could continue to live on the scale to which she was accustomed, she would not concern herself with how that scale was maintained, nor at what cost to her husband's peace of mind.

'Is there any way I can help?'

Touched, Richard patted her hand paternally. 'It's nothing that need bother your little head, sweetheart. But thank you for caring enough to ask.'

She gave him a doubtful smile, suppressing a sigh of frustration. Her father was a dear, but even he was determined to keep her wrapped in cotton wool, as if she were so fragile that she would shatter at the harsh touch of reality. There seemed little point in pursuing this rather useless train of thought; she began a sprightly if artificial conversation with Donald Farquharson, a business associate of Richard's, on some of the new types of ski bindings.

After dinner, coffee and liqueurs were served in the lounge. Almost immediately Boyd came up to her, bringing a glass of her favourite Tia Maria. With none of his customary circumlocution, he said flatly, 'I won't accept that you mean "no", Rana. It's been a big adjustment for you coming home again, and you're understandably tired and confused. I have to go to Calgary tomorrow to attend some special court sessions, but I'll be back by the weekend and we can discuss it further then.'

'Rana, how nice to see you again! And Boyd, you're looking well.'

It was Mrs Charmian Raymond, a henna-haired and loquacious bridge partner of Dorothea's, who had an all-consuming interest in other people's affairs. Now she coyly patted Rana on the arm, her sharp little eyes unabashedly searching for her ring finger. 'What, no diamond yet?' she catechised. She shook her little finger, adorned with an emerald so large as to be vulgar, in Boyd's face. 'Haven't you popped the question yet, Boyd?'

For once Boyd was at a loss for words. Acutely embarrassed, Rana was almost relieved when Dorothea joined them.

'Well, Dorothea,' Charmian rattled on roguishly, 'I had hoped to congratulate you on a prospective new son-in-law this evening. Why, you yourself led me to believe an engagement was in the wind.'

Even as Dorothea shot a vitriolic glance at her daughter, Rana saw Heath Markland approaching, soft-footed on the thick carpet, and quite near enough to have overheard Charmian's shrill-voiced remarks. It was the final straw.

Nevertheless, she was unaware of the naked appeal in her face until he spoke. 'Good evening, Miss Liscombe,' he said, the gleam in his eye mocking his own formality. 'There's some rather delectable dance music playing in the sunroom. Won't you join me?'

Before she could say a word, he had firmly tucked her ice-cold hand into his sleeve and had led her away. Blindly she followed him to the sunroom, where four other couples were sedately circling on the polished hardwood floor to the lilting melody of an old-fashioned Strauss waltz. Heath put one arm firmly about her waist, turning her so that she faced him. Staring up at him, a lump of unshed tears in her throat, Rana faltered, 'Thank you—for rescuing me, I mean.'

His expression was unreadable. 'Any time,' he said coolly. 'And now, don't talk. Just dance.' His lean fingers encircled her hand, giving it warmth, and he drew her closer to his hard body. At first she followed his lead automatically, but then gradually the tension seeped from her limbs and unconsciously she relaxed, her slender form pliant in his hold. She loved dancing, and to her inward pleasure he was an expert; her body swayed gracefully to every nuance of the music's stirring rhythm. But all the time she was acutely conscious of the brush of his thigh against hers, and of the sinewy strength of the arm around her waist; to her nostrils drifted the subtly masculine aroma of shaving lotion and tobacco and warm, clean skin.

A fierce longing seized her to lay her cheek against his shoulder and mould her limbs to his, giving herself up to the sensual pleasure of his embrace: thoughts which flushed her cheeks with delicate colour and gentled the vivid blue of her eyes to pansy darkness. Twice during the evening this tall stranger had been sensitive to her distress in a way that neither her parents nor Boyd had been, and had delivered her from potentially embarrassing situations. He seemed to have penetrated to her very soul with his incisive grey eyes. Yet when they had first met yesterday, she had borne the brunt of his stinging mockery . . .

They executed a complicated turn in perfect unison, and she laughed up at him in sheer delight. He appraised her upturned face seriously. 'Feeling better?'

'Mmm—much.'

'Good. You look better ... I told you you need some colour in your cheeks.'

Temper flared in her face, deeping its flush. 'Oh? And do people always do as you tell them, Mr Markland?'

'It's usually to their advantage to do so,' he replied, an edge of steel in his even voice, so that she shivered slightly.

'So you like power,' she murmured provocatively.

'I control my own destiny, Rana—you can call that power if you like.'

'I'd call it pride ... or arrogance.'

'Would you? But then I didn't expect you to understand. It's painfully obvious you have absolutely no control over your life.'

She gasped with outrage, forgetting that a few minutes ago she had been grateful for his sensitivity towards her. 'Allow me to add rudeness to my description of you!' she snapped.

With swift steps he danced her to the corner of the room furthest from the light and then stopped, holding her so firmly that she could hardly move. His eyes bored into hers. 'At least be honest with yourself, Rana, even if you can't be with me or anyone else. Your mother rules your life and you know it.'

'I thought you were a lumberman, not a psychiatrist,' she stormed childishly.

'Who chose your dress?' He gave it a single disparaging glance that spoke volumes.

'My mother did. But——'

'Who suggested that hairstyle?'

'Since you seem to know all the answers, why don't you tell me?'

'I don't have to—we both know who did. You have beautiful hair, what a shame to torture it into that tangle of curls. How old are you?'

'I don't have to answer all your questions!'

'I would have thought that was a fairly straightforward one.'

'I'm twenty,' she said sullenly.

'Then isn't it time you started doing some things you want to do?'

His question was unanswerable, for it found too many echoes in her own mind. She bit her lip in vexation.

'Rana!'

Rana jumped. 'That's my mother, I'll have to go.'

'Exactly.'

She stamped her foot angrily, and one of her carefully arranged ringlets tumbled free, to lie in a silken curl against her neck. Heath reached up and deliberately twisted it around his finger, his hand stroking her neck with leisurely sensuality. Weakness invaded her limbs, so that she had the overwhelming urge to run her own fingers through his thick blond hair. Horrified by compulsions that were new to her and whose source she did not understand, she pulled away, leaving a few pale strands entangled in his hand.

'We haven't finished our conversation,' he said with soft menace. 'I'll see you later.'

'Not if I can help it!'

She hurriedly left the room, and the next hour passed in a blur of polite chit-chat and duty dances with husbands of her mother's friends. Then to her relief she realised that people were beginning to leave; at last the dreadful evening was drawing to a close.

Boyd was among the first to get his coat. 'Early start tomorrow, darling,' he said with prosaic good sense that was so characteristic of him. Before she could avoid him, he planted a deft kiss on her lips. 'I'll see you when I get back. Take care of yourself, and get some rest.'

She nodded dumbly, wishing that her rebellion could be cured by something as simple as a good night's sleep. Out of the corner of her eye she saw Charmian bearing down on them, and said distractedly, 'Goodbye, Boyd.

Have a good trip,' before fleeing to the deserted dining-room. She shut the door behind her and leaned against the panels, closing her eyes, as a wave of unaccountable depression washed over her.

'Where were we?'

Her eyelids snapped open. Heath Markland emerged from the shadows of an alcove and sauntered towards her, moving with an animal grace that both fascinated and disturbed her.

'I thought you'd gone,' she said with scant civility.

'Now who's being rude?'

She shrugged, too tired and unhappy to care what he thought of her.

Imperceptibly his voice changed. 'Go upstairs and put on some blue jeans—I trust you own some, or does your mother disapprove of them too?—and a sweater. We're going for a walk.'

'For a walk?'

'That's what I said.'

'You're crazy! It's past midnight.'

'So what?'

'But——'

He surveyed her soberly across the width of the room, and when he spoke his words were oddly gentle. 'Rana, have you never done crazy things on the spur of the moment? Gone for a walk in the moonlight, or run barefoot through the wet grass, or watched the sun come up behind the mountains?'

She shook her head silently.

'Then it's high time you started. Go and change ... and don't worry, I'll handle your family.'

Feeling as though she were in a dream, Rana did as she was told. The only pair of jeans she could find in her cupboard dated from a couple of years ago; as she pulled them on, she discovered she must have put on a little weight in the interim, for they clung to the curve of her hips and slim length of her legs with rather startling fidelity. She donned a thin white turtleneck and over it a soft green mohair sweater ... no time to do anything with her hair, so she tied a green and white silk scarf over it, knotting it at the nape of her neck. She did not realise how becoming this looked, highlighting the perfect lines of her cheekbones and the thick fringe of her lashes. Running down the stairs two at a time, she found Heath waiting for her in the hall; no one else was in sight.

'Well,' he said slowly, running his eyes up and down her slender figure, 'that's more like it. Are you ready?'

'Does someone know we're leaving?' she faltered.

'Your grandfather thought my idea was excellent. Your mother was unfortunately detained by some of her guests, but he'll tell her where we've gone. Let's go.'

They slipped out into the warm darkness, Heath's hand on her elbow as he guided her down the path towards his car, a low-slung black sports model. He seemed disinclined for conversation, so in silence they drove along with the river bank towards the heart of the city, still noisy with traffic, and spangled with streetlights and flashing neon signs. Finally she ventured, 'Where are we going?'

'To my hotel.'

She stiffened. 'You said we were going for a walk!'

'Relax, Rana,' he said soothingly, removing one hand from the wheel to pat her denim-clad knee ... as though she were ten years old, she fumed. Yet her annoyance could not quite quell the beginnings of panic. A man did not take a girl to his hotel in the middle of the night to talk about the weather, she was not that naïve; especially not a man like Heath Markland, she thought, stealing a glance at his implacable profile. His chiselled lips held more than a hint of sensuality, she now realised, increasingly aware of the intense masculinity of his broad-shouldered, well-muscled frame. His hands clasped the wheel lightly; they were strong, capable hands, lean yet shapely, and in spite of herself she recalled the delicious lassitude his touch induced in her. Only too well could she remember the steely strength of his embrace as they had danced, knowing that if he chose to force himself upon her, she would be virtually defenceless. Forgetting her pride, she said in a small voice, 'Why are we going to your hotel?'

He glanced at her, the glow of light from the dashboard casting angular shadows on his inscrutable face. 'My dear girl, I'm not about to seduce you, if that's what you are worrying about—or was it rape you had in mind?' He laughed derisively. 'I like my women willing . . . and sophisticated enough to know the score.'

Hurt and rage warred in her breast. 'You really are despicable!'

Skilfully he swung the car into a parking space on a side street and turned off the ignition. 'We're going to my hotel so I can change my clothes. And then we're going for a walk. So you can stop contemplating a fate worse than death. Lock your door, will you?'

There was no sense in arguing. A two-minute walk and they were approaching the lobby of one of the few hotels in Edmonton to which her mother gave her unqualified approval. He marched her across the vast hush of the chandeliered, thickly carpeted lobby to the elevators, and allowed an impressively uniformed bellboy to conduct them to the twelfth floor. There Heath produced a door key and ushered her into his room . . . more thick carpet, long velvet drapes, and an immense high-postered bed from which she hurriedly averted her eyes. An antique mirror adorned one of the oak-panelled walls, and belatedly Rana's sense of the ridiculous surfaced.

Purposely she drew Heath in front of it: it reflected an image of a slim, laughing girl in shabby jeans, and a tall debonair man in formal evening attire. 'I hope you —and the bellboy—realised that you're escorting Edmonton's best-dressed woman of the year!'

His eyes met hers on the mirror's surface and for the second time she was the recipient of his warm, unforced smile, a smile that lightened the harsh outlines of his features, took ten years off his age, and also—she fumbled in her mind for the right word—made him seem somehow vulnerable. 'How old are you?' she demanded peremptorily, only realising after the words were spoken that it was not the sort of question a sophisticated woman 'who knew the score' would ask.

'Thirty-four.'

Still gazing at him in the mirror, for she lacked the courage to confront him face to face, she said, 'You should smile like that more often.'

His softly spoken reply expressed an implicit challenge. 'Perhaps that's partly up to you, Rana?'

'That sounds like passing the buck.'

'I think not.' As he spoke, he was peeling off his jacket, throwing it carelessly on the bed, and was fumbling with the catch on his bow tie. In quick impatience he grunted, 'Undo this damn thing for me, will you? I had the devil's own time getting it on.'

He sat on the edge of the bed and bent his head forward. He could not have seen the faint hesitation in her manner as she approached him nor the slight tremor in her fingers. The back of his neck was firmly corded with muscles, his thick unruly hair curling against the tanned skin. Her palm brushed the warmth of his flesh and she could feel the heat of the contact spread throughout her body, until she was sure he must sense it. Awkwardly she eased the gold clasp free of the tiny buttonhole and loosened the tie, then stepped back quickly.

'Thanks.' He stood up, discarding the tie with the jacket, and beginning to undo the buttons of his starched white shirt; there was a tangle of gold hair on the smooth brown skin of his chest. She dragged her eyes away to find his intent gaze full upon her flushed cheeks and parted lips. He made a quick move towards her, then just as suddenly dropped his arms to his sides, expelling his breath in a tiny hiss between his teeth. Turning his back to her, he took clothes from the cupboard and said as casually as if those charged moments of tension between them had never occurred, 'I'll only be a minute,' and disappeared into the bathroom.

Rana took a deep breath, trying to quieten the quickened beat of her heart. Had he touched her, as she was almost certain he had wanted to, how would she have responded? She would never know now . . . restlessly she wandered over to the desk; she was idly flipping through the pages of a magazine when he reappeared.

She had seen him yesterday in a dark business suit and this evening in a tuxedo, and he had worn both with a feline grace and authority. But now, in tight fitting brown corduroy trousers and an off-white sweater, worn leather boots on his feet, he looked perfectly at ease, more at home with himself, the casual clothes emphasising his vibrant maleness and good looks.

'Ready?' he said brusquely. With a sinking heart she saw that the steel was back in his eyes, their momentary contact a thing of the past. In silence she preceded him from the room and they descended in the elevator, the bell-boy regarding them with a lack of surprise that must, she supposed, be part of his stock-in-trade as a hotel employee.

In the car Heath snapped a cassette in the tape deck, the flow of music making conversation unnecessary. Well, Rana thought indignantly, two can play that game! So she leaned back in the comfortable bucket seat, closing her eyes. She must have dozed off briefly; for in what seemed a very brief time, she felt the car bumping over a rough track and coming to a halt. 'Where are we?' she murmured in confusion.

'You'll see,' was the uncompromising reply.

She got out of the car, stretching with unselfconscious grace. As she grew accustomed to the darkness, she discovered that they were standing at the edge of a field, bordered by a few pine and overgrown alders. A soft breeze stirred against her skin, carrying with it the sweet scent of long green grass and wildflowers.

Heath swung open the barred gate, its protesting

screech incredibly loud against the night's velvet silence. Together they strolled down the lane, where the moon cast eerie shadows across their path. Eventually they came to an old wooden fence and leaned on the top bar, gazing across the meadowland to the distant hills in the west; through no conscious effort of Rana's will, all the accumulated strife and anxiety of the day slowly seeped from her body, to be replaced by the serenity of a world very remote from her own. For the first time since she had come home she felt at peace with herself, the restlessness of her spirit appeased by the space and freedom of her surroundings.

If someone had told her that morning that she would end the day walking in the moonlight with a man she had not yet met, she would have been convinced they were crazy, she thought. Yet it seemed entirely natural to be here with Heath, sharing a silence that for the moment at least held no undercurrents of hostility.

She glanced up at her companion. His eyes seemed to be focussed on the far horizon, although she would have sworn he was blind to the beauty of the hills; his visions were inward, and from his haggard features and tightly held mouth, she divined that they were far from happy ones. Wanting only to bring him back to the present, she said tentatively, 'Heath . . .?'

He started visibly. 'Oh . . . sorry, Rana, I was miles away. What did you say?'

'I guess I just wanted to say thank you for bringing me here,' she said shyly.

He raised his eyebrows. 'Don't tell me you've never been out this way before?'

'No . . . never,' she confessed. 'I—I've never done anything like this before either—gone for a walk in the country after a dance, I mean. Just on the spur of the moment.' She gave a tiny laugh of sheer wonderment. 'It's fun!'

'You sound as though you've been brought up in a convent.'

'Well, hardly. Although my parents are pretty strict. Perhaps if I'd had brothers and sisters, things would have been different.' There was an underlying thread of loneliness in her voice, for when she had been a child her father had often been away on business and her mother absorbed in her social pursuits, so that the blonde-haired little girl had been left to devise her own solitary amusements.

'How long are you going to use that for an excuse?'

Her head jerked up, for his question had been unwontedly sharp. 'An excuse for what?'

'For the fact that at the age of twenty, you have no idea how to direct your own life. You're just a pawn in your family's hands. Isn't it time you took control?'

It was one thing for her to think these things, but quite another for Heath Markland to hurl them at her. 'I fail to see that it's any of your business,' she replied as quellingly as possible.

'Perhaps I intend to make it my business. In which case, my dear Rana, neither you nor anyone else will stop me.'

Frightened by the threat implicit in his words, Rana said as calmly as she could, 'This seems a pointless discussion. I think it's time we went home.'

'Not quite.'

He moved nearer. Before she could evade him, one hand encircled her waist, drawing her closer, and the other seized her hand, almost as though they were dancing again. Her heart began to beat with slow, heavy strokes. Her eyes, pools of darkness in her translucent skin, widened in panic. She tried to twist free, but his big body held her a prisoner. Then his mouth claimed hers. Softly, gently, with a tenderness belied by his steel grip, his lips quested and searched hers, drowning fears in a rising tide of sensation totally new to her. She lost her tautness, relaxing against him in unconscious surrender, her breasts soft against the muscled hardness of his chest.

He drew back and she gave a tiny moan of protest. Then his cynical words struck her trembling frame like a whiplash. 'You really are a little innocent, aren't you? I wasn't far wrong when I said you could have been brought up in a convent. Your mother should be taken to task for letting you loose on the world.'

All the bittersweet longing his kiss had aroused transformed itself instantly into fury. 'Why don't you try leaving my mother out of it for five minutes?' she spat.

'Why—so you can avoid the issue?'

'You've already made the real issue quite clear—you like your women experienced. Those were your exact words, I believe.'

His fingers closed about her wrist like an iron trap. 'Experience can be quickly gained, my dear.'

'Let go of me!'

'Such a temper under that cool, touch-me-not exterior! Maybe there is some hope for you.'

A glorious sweep of anger rid her of the last of her inhibitions. 'Just what the hell are you trying to prove?' she cried, her breast heaving with emotion, twin flags of colour raised on her cheekbones.

His own anger rose to clash with hers. 'That there's a real human being buried somewhere under all the layers of convention and good manners and pretty speeches you hide behind.'

Goaded beyond caution, she swung her free hand up with all her strength to strike his cheek. Not even taking his eyes from her face, in lightning-swift reaction he imprisoned her wrist. 'Nice girls don't hit their escorts, Miss Liscombe,' he mocked. 'Hasn't your mother ever told you that?'

'You're insufferable!' she seethed, fighting for self-control. 'Now will you please let go and take me home immediately.'

'One thing you might as well find out about me right now, Rana—I don't take orders.'

'Of course not. You're only interested in giving them,

and making sure they're obeyed. Anyway, I don't care. After tonight, I don't want ever to see you again.'

'Come on now,' he chided. 'Admit that in half an hour with me you've learned more than in a dozen dates with your friend Boyd Dexter.'

'Keep him out of this!'

'Allow me to give you a word of advice—don't let your mother talk you into marrying him, will you?'

He was so close to the truth that she could think of nothing to say.

'I see I'm right,' he said with a satisfied air. 'Just let me ask you two questions, Rana, and then I'll take you home—has Boyd ever kissed you as I did this evening?' His voice husky, hypnotising her to immobility, he went on, 'And have you ever felt before tonight the fire I lit in your veins, so that you wanted the kiss to go on for ever, until your whole body drowned in desire?'

Struck to her soul by his words, and impotent to fight him any longer, she felt her lip tremble and a sheen of tears blur her vision. 'Please,' she quavered, 'I want to go home.'

He released her wrists, and absently she rubbed them to restore her circulation; they would be black and blue tomorrow, for like most fair-skinned people she bruised easily. Irrelevantly she wondered how she would explain them to Eli.

'Come on.'

Dumbly she followed him back to the car and sat in stony silence all the way home. He pulled up in front of the darkened house and reached across her to open the car door. His violence had dissipated itself and he was again in complete control of himself. 'Think over what I said, Rana,' he said quietly. With one finger he traced the line of her cheek to the corner of her mouth. 'You're a woman of courage and integrity—don't let yourself be trapped into anything that isn't right for you. You can be as free as you want to be.'

His gentleness, so unexpected, robbed her of the last of

her precarious composure. 'Oh, stop!' she cried raggedly. 'Leave me alone! I never want to see you again!' She slammed the door and ran for the house, his soft-spoken 'goodnight' echoing in her ears.

CHAPTER TWO

It was past ten when Rana woke the next morning. She lay still in the wide bed, reluctant to get up and start the day, because even though she wouldn't have to see Boyd, there was still her mother to face ... but she could at least postpone that confrontation until this afternoon, since she was having lunch with Eli; he could be depended upon to give her a sympathetic ear.

As soon as she got up, she washed her hair, ridding herself of the despised ringlets. Once it was dry, she pulled it back into a smooth chignon—not a curl in sight, she thought with a wry grin at herself in the mirror. As she applied her make-up, she wondered what to wear ... not the grey dress, for she was fairly sure Eli would agree with Heath Markland's estimation of that.

Heath Markland—unwillingly she allowed the memory to surface of their moonlight walk just a few brief hours ago. She remembered the easy, loping grace of his tall figure, the bruising hardness of his body against hers, the languorous arousal of his kiss that had, she realised in wonderment, transformed her from an innocent, unawakened girl to a woman. For the first time in her life she had felt the devastating power of passion and desire; the longing for fulfilment in a man's arms had swept away all the fears and cautions so carefully instilled in her by her mother.

With painful honesty Rana looked deep into her heart and recognised that she did not love Boyd, nor would she ever love him. Since last night it had become inconceivable that she could marry anyone who did not inspire that wanton fire in her blood, that primitive urge for closeness and surrender. Until Heath Markland had kissed her, she had not known such feelings existed dormant within her. Perhaps he had been cruel to awaken her so violently ... but perhaps his very ruthlessness had been a kindness.

Furthermore, the claustrophobic restlessness she had tried so hard to deny was a reality; the arrogant Heath Markland had shown her that too. What was it he had said? 'You are a woman of courage and integrity. Don't let yourself be trapped.' Somehow she had to act on his words, leave home and establish herself independently; a thrill of excitement kindled within her at the thought. She would ask Eli for advice. And possibly, just possibly, she would ask Eli to convey to Heath Markland her thanks for all he had taught her.

Hastily she flipped through the dresses in her closet, most of which had been chosen under Dorothea's eagle eye. Then, almost at the back, she found a peasant-style skirt in cherry-red corduroy dotted with tiny flowers, its red cummerbund snug about her waist. Teamed with a crisp white blouse and tight-fitting knee-high leather boots, it looked stylish and eye-catching. She twirled to see the back and the flared skirt swung provocatively around her legs. Purposely avoiding her mother's domain, Rana ran down the back stairs, and backed her car out of the garage. For at least an hour she was free ...

Having parked the car, she was too impatient to wait for the elevator, so she ran up the stairs towards Eli's office, still filled with a strange sense of joie de vivre. Panting from the climb, she turned the corner and collided head-on with the man who had been running equally rapidly down the stairs. All the breath knocked from her body, she reeled backwards, only to be caught and held in a vice-like grip with which she was all too familiar. It was Heath Markland. Her eyes widened in shock, then her lashes fluttered down to hide their brilliant azure. Her heartbeat quickened.

The silence stretched from seconds to minutes, until finally Rana looked up, surprising a spark of some indefinable emotion in the narrowed, smoke-grey eyes ... the look of a hunter who sees his prey?

'You're looking very beautiful,' he said, a rough note in his voice that she had not heard before.

'Thank you,' she answered simply. Her mind seemed to have gone completely blank.

'I'm taking you out for lunch.'

His cool assumption of authority immediately irritated her. She raised her chin and said coolly, 'No, you're not.'

'Rana, one of these days you'll contradict me once too often. Where do you want to eat?'

'I'm having lunch with Eli.'

'Eli had to go to a board meeting, so he asked me to deputise. He didn't think you'd mind.'

'Well, he was wrong,' she said crossly.

'Why?'

'Because I don't like the way you're always telling me what to do.'

'Miss Liscombe,' he said with a mocking bow, 'please will you do me the honour of having lunch with me?'

She glared at him, certain that once again he was laughing at her. 'I've already told you I don't want to,' she said firmly, although inwardly she was not at all sure this was the truth.

With uncanny perception he must have divined her thoughts. 'Nonsense.' Grabbing her hand, he steered her towards the stairs. 'We'll go to Le Marmiton.'

In spite of herself, her fingers nestled within his handclasp, and she knew further resistance was beyond her. 'All right,' she said meekly.

As they walked the five or six blocks to the restaurant, Rana soon learned that even a stroll on city streets could hold adventure with Heath Markland. He was apt to stop and investigate anything that caught his attention and he expected her to exhibit the same intense interest, be it in a display of books, Western saddles, or antique furniture. She discovered that his knowledge was both wide-ranging and far from superficial, and he was so genuinely interested in what she had to say that she heard herself expressing opinions she had scarcely known she held, and exhibiting the flashing wit that usually she shared only with Eli.

They came to a sidewalk flower stand and Heath stopped. The cart was loaded with carnations, daisies, roses and violets, droplets of water sparkling on the vivid petals. Carefully Heath selected half a dozen creamy white long-stemmed roses, then added to them six more deep red ones; he paid the proprietor, then handed Rana the sheaf of blossoms. She looked up at him, a smile tugging at the corner of her mouth. 'They're lovely—thank you.'

'The symbolism is rather obvious, I'm afraid, but it's the best I can do.'

Doubtfully she repeated, 'Symbolism?'

He touched a tightly curled white bud. 'To most people you're like this—cool, remote, beautiful but untouchable ... and untouched.' One of the red roses had unfurled its velvet petals, and holding it up, Heath went on, 'But this is the real you, Rana. Warm and open and passionate.'

She was suddenly terrified out of all proportion by the vibrant conviction in his tone; could he be right, and all the others—her mother and father and Boyd—be wrong?

As though he had read her mind, Heath said quietly, 'It's a risk to be like the red rose, Rana. You can be badly hurt, for to expose yourself is to be vulnerable. But it's the only way your life will mean anything.'

He sounded so convincing. Perplexed and still obscurely frightened, Rana buried her face in the fragrant flowers. 'I hope they won't wilt before I get them home,' she said, determined to change the subject to something safer; even as she spoke she sensed he was disappointed by her evasion.

'It's no great loss if they do,' he said ironically. 'Just ask Boyd to buy you more. I imagine he always does what he's told. He bought you the pale pink ones you wore last night, didn't he? Just what I'd expect.'

'Whatever his faults, Boyd is my friend,' she said sharply, glad of the chance to get away from the subject of roses.

'Your loyalty does you credit,' was the dry response. 'Here's the restaurant. I hope you're hungry.'

She preceded him into the attractive dining room, its decor that of an old French Canadian inn; although she felt faintly foolish clutching the armload of roses, she was also conscious of a twinge of pride in her escort, very much aware of how the eyes of several women noticed his height and arrogant masculinity. They were soon seated by the window, and in fluent French Heath rapidly dealt with the menu. At her raised eyebrows he said, 'I lived in a lumber camp in northern Quebec for a couple of years, that's where I learned to speak French. Not all of us can go to finishing school in Switzerland.'

She glowered at him. 'If you want to spoil my appetite, you're going about it the right way!'

Incredibly he laughed, his teeth white against his tanned face. 'I'm sorry, Rana, there was no need for me to say that.'

Disarmed by his apology, she said, 'Tell me about yourself, Heath. Where you grew up, where you live now, whether you have any brothers or sisters—I really don't know anything about you.' Except, an inner voice whispered, that I feel so alive when I'm with you, and I notice every change of expression in your face, and your nearness both scares and excites me.

His face clouded, as he stared down at the tablecloth, his long fingers absently rearranging the cutlery. 'There's not much to tell,' he said slowly. 'My parents died when I was only five. I hardly remember them—just the occasional recollection of a big bearded man who always seemed to be laughing, and of a tiny, delicate woman ... her colouring was much like yours, and she was beautiful, too. She used to sing around the house while she worked. We lived up north because my father hated cities ... there was a bad 'flu epidemic one winter and the doctor couldn't get there in time, so my mother died. Three weeks later my father was killed in a log jam on the river; I suppose his grief had made him careless. The wilderness can be a cruel place, there's no room for mistakes.'

Touched to the heart by this bleak narrative, Rana put her hand over Heath's; it was the first time she had voluntarily touched him. Her blue eyes liquid with sympathy, she said gently, 'I'm so sorry.'

He stared at her fingers, so slender and feminine in contrast to his. 'Oh, it's a long time ago now. But it taught me a lesson I've never forgotten—to seize life while you can, for there's no certainty in anything—life, love, happiness—they can be taken from you as capriciously as they're given.'

'Surely not?' she said in distress. 'There must be a plan, a purpose to it all.'

'I'd like to believe that. But I don't think you can depend on anything ... or anyone, Rana. So take what you can today and don't waste time worrying about tomorrow.'

She fell silent, certain he was wrong yet unable to put her conviction into words. 'So what happened to you after your parents died, Heath? Where did you go?'

'We went to live with my grandfather in the Peace River country, where he owned vast holdings of woodland. Lumbering's been in my blood for three generations.'

'We?' she queried.

'My brother and I.' His face closed.

'I see.' Not wanting to pry, but intensely curious to

hear more, she said, 'Your grandfather was a friend of Eli's, wasn't he?'

'Yes, that's right. In fact they were business partners. It was a pretty lonely life up there in the cabin at Clearwater. We had few friends, so we cherished the ones we had. Whenever he came, Eli brought us boys a big box of chocolates and a book. He's a fine man, your grandfather.'

There was a finality in his last statement that seemed to end the reminiscences of his childhood. Tentatively she asked, 'So where do you live now? Not in Edmonton?'

'No!' he answered vehemently, then laughed at his own forcefulness. 'I guess I must have inherited my father's dislike of cities. Fine places to visit, but not to live in. A man needs room to breathe ... no, I still live at Clearwater, although not in the old cabin. I built myself a house on the edge of the lake.' At her look of enquiry, he went on, 'Clearwater's about fifteen miles north of Rexton. I usually fly from Edmonton to Rexton, it's a couple of hundred miles, then I take the jeep into Clearwater. There is a road, of sorts.'

There was something in the way he talked about Clearwater that prompted her to say, 'Tell me more about your home.'

'Clearwater ...' he mused. 'It's a big, crescent-shaped lake, one of a chain. On windless days its surface is like glass, and the water so crystal clear you can see the trout swimming near the bottom. The forest grows right to the shoreline, so you can always hear birds singing. Loons nest on it in the summer, and most days deer and caribou and moose come to drink. When I built the house I only cleared an acre or so; I wanted the wilderness all around me.'

Fascinated, wishing she could see it with her own eyes, she asked, 'But aren't there any other people?'

'Not very many. There's my housekeeper, and an old fellow who keeps an eye on the buildings and grounds for me, that's all. Of course all the lumber camps are scattered in a twenty mile radius and I have radio communication with them.'

'It must be very isolated in winter.'

'Yeah.' He shrugged. 'I like it that way. The foremen from the camps drop in a lot, and in summer friends come to stay.'

Rana couldn't help wondering how many of the friends were women; he did not look the type of man to live a celibate life. She was roused from these thoughts to hear him say, 'I'm going back home later this afternoon. Why don't you come with me for the weekend?'

Her jaw dropped inelegantly, so unexpected was this invitation. 'Oh—I couldn't.'

'Don't you want to see it?'

'Well, yes,' she said honestly, 'I do.'

'Then what's the problem?'

'Heath, I hardly know you. I can't just go away with you for the weekend.' Her troubled eyes looked squarely at him, flinching at the challenge in his face.

'It's a chance for you to break out of your cage, Rana. Risk it and come with me . . . I'll take you canoeing in the moonlight and fishing at dawn. I'll show you a beaver dam and bear cubs and a family of goslings.' Deliberately he let his eyes wander over the delicate beauty of her face, the soft swell of her breasts under the tight jumper. 'I'm not saying I won't kiss you or touch you—but I'll do nothing against your will, that I do promise.'

His ruthless honesty set her heart pounding in her breast. She wanted to go with him, to accept his challenge, more than she had ever wanted anything in her life. Yet she was afraid. If she went with Heath Markland, nothing would ever be the same again. Moreover, she was frightened of the sheer physical attraction he had for her. Remembering how eagerly she had responded to the touch of his lips, she wondered if she would be able to temper her body's treacherous longing for his. How could she control forces she scarcely understood, primitive elemental drives that paid no attention to the careful dictates of her conventional upbringing?

'I'm offering you change and adventure and excitement,' he persisted softly.

But not safety, she thought. Not security or kindness... or tenderness. Her eyes lingered on his implacable mouth and slate grey eyes. Had he ever given tenderness and love to a woman? It did not seem very likely. He was a hard man, whose rough life would not have taught him the gentler virtues. Her stomach tightened with apprehension; there was only one answer she could give. Without conscious volition she shook her head.

'So you won't come—you're a coward, Rana.'

'I'm not!' she denied, all the more fiercely because she was afraid it was true.

'Yes, you are. You're scared to step outside your safe little world in case you can't find your way back. You're no granddaughter of Eli's, Rana—you're your mother's daughter.' He signalled for the bill and dismissively pushed back his chair. 'I'll take you to your car.'

Tears gathered in her eyes and she blinked them away, determined not to cry in front of him. They left the restaurant and walked back the way they had come, but this time they did not tarry to chat in front of every window; she almost had to run to keep up with his angry, long-legged strides. He led her up the narrow stairs to the ramp where her car was parked, the ugly concrete building inducing in her the same claustrophobic sense of suffocation that it had yesterday.

'Which car is yours?'

'The blue one, over there.'

He took the keys from her nerveless fingers and unlocked the door, holding it open for her, his tightly leashed anger all too evident to the girl, sensitive as she was to his every mood. In a blinding flash of despair it suddenly became clear to her that if she got in her car and drove away, she would never see Heath Markland again. He was too proud a man to beg. He would disappear from her life as abruptly as he had entered it and she would never know what the future might have held for her had she gone with him.

'What are you waiting for?' he demanded. He flicked her bouquet of roses with an impatient finger. 'Keep the white roses, Rana—but make sure you throw away the red ones. It's obvious they're not for you.'

Deep within her, the last core of resistance shattered. From a long distance away she heard her voice say ungraciously, 'All right, you win! I'll go with you to Clearwater.'

He betrayed not the slightest flicker of reaction. 'What time can you be ready?'

'Whenever you like,' she replied recklessly.

'I'll pick you up in an hour.'

She had herself under better control now, and as she got into her car, said with commendable calm, 'That'll be fine.'

'Good. I'll see you later.' He gave her a brief unsmiling salute, before striding away.

She started the car and drove off, not even allowing herself a backward glance at his tall figure. Driving home rather faster than usual, she automatically obeyed the stop lights and avoided the other traffic. It was not until she had parked the car in the garage and gathered up her handbag and the bunch of roses that the full enormity of what she had done struck her. She had agreed to spend the weekend with a man she had known scarcely twenty-four hours, a man to whom she felt herself dangerously attracted. She must have been out of her mind to say she'd go! Somehow she'd have to get out of it . . .

'Rana! Is that you?' Dorothea called from the house.

Mentally bracing herself, Rana cried, 'Coming!' and ran up the stairs to the side door.

Dorothea was in the front hall tending the flower

arrangements from the night before. 'How was your lunch?' she asked.

'Oh, fine.'

'Did Eli say whether or not he'd be coming for dinner?'

'Well, as a matter of fact, I didn't see him. He was tied up at a board meeting and couldn't make it for lunch.'

'Oh? Did you eat alone, then?'

'No—no, I didn't.'

'Don't tell me you ended up eating with his secretary. No doubt a very worthy woman, but so dreadfully dull.'

'She's very pleasant, Mother,' Rana contradicted, and then, incurably truthful, added, 'But no, I didn't. I had lunch with Mr Markland.'

Dorothea put down the chrysanthemum she had been trimming and said sharply, 'And no doubt he gave you that ridiculous bunch of flowers?'

Rana looked down at the roses, their long stems and heavy heads already wilting. 'They need water.'

'Rana,' her mother said with deceptive gentleness, 'I think we need to have a little talk. I can see how a man like Heath Markland could have an unsettling effect on a young girl like you—he's attractive in a rough sort of way, and quite different from anyone you've ever met. But I am certainly not going to allow him to jeopardise your future in any way. I want you to promise not to see him again.' Plainly not expecting any opposition, she inserted the big yellow bloom into the vase and pulled out another.

'What don't you like about him?' Rana asked rebelliously.

'My dear, he's a nobody,' Dorothea said, surprised anyone could ask such an obvious question. 'Oh, he's rich enough, I suppose, but his social background is deplorable—both his father and his grandfather were nothing but common lumbermen.'

'There are those who might say the same of Eli! But

that's beside the point, isn't it? Mother, I'm twenty years old. Don't you think I should be able to choose my own friends?'

She had Dorothea's whole attention now. 'If your choice is someone like Heath Markland, then obviously not! I was very annoyed when I heard you'd gone out with him last night, especially after the disgraceful way you treated Boyd. Well, at least Boyd will be back tomorrow. I've invited him for dinner, by the way. Just consider yourself lucky that he's giving you a second chance.'

'I don't want a second chance! I told Boyd I couldn't marry him, and I meant it,' Rana replied in growing agitation. 'We wouldn't be happy together, Mother, don't you see that? I don't love him.'

'I simply don't understand you since you've come home from Switzerland; you've changed, and much for the worse. You were always so tractable. But now your head seems to be stuffed with a lot of romantic nonsense. Of course you and Boyd are ideally suited for each other, and tomorrow evening you can tell him so.'

Rana took a deep, steadying breath. 'I won't be here tomorrow evening.'

'What do you mean?' Dorothea demanded in staccato tones.

'Heath Markland has invited me to his home in the Peace River area. We're leaving as soon as he comes for me.'

'And when were you thinking of coming back?'

Heath hadn't mentioned a time for their return, Rana now realised. Weakly she said, 'Well, I'm not sure. On Sunday, I suppose.'

'I forbid you to go!'

Ten minutes ago Rana had decided she couldn't possibly spend the weekend with Heath, and now her mother had presented her with the perfect excuse: all she had to do was tell him she was not allowed to go. Then in her mind his deep voice echoed and re-echoed,

'Don't let yourself be trapped, Rana ... you can be free ... I'll take you canoeing in the moonlight ... I'll give you excitement and adventure ...'

Speaking as unemotionally as she could, the girl said, 'Mother, please listen to me for a minute and try to understand. I can't marry Boyd—I'm sorry, but that's all there is to it. You're right, I guess I have changed. Boyd is a nice man and I'm fond of him, but there has to be more to marriage than that. And there's really no harm in me going with Heath. Eli will vouch for him, I know —his grandfather and Eli were friends.'

'I repeat—you are not going anywhere with Heath Markland!'

'Mother——'

'There's nothing more to say, Rana. Go upstairs and change, and then you can help me with the rest of the flowers. Your father won't be home for dinner this evening, so I thought after we've finished here we'd go downtown and do a little shopping.'

'For my trousseau?' Rana asked with barely disguised irony.

Interpreting this as acquiescence, Dorothea said, 'That's right, dear.'

'For the last time, Mother, I won't marry Boyd! And I am going to Clearwater with Heath.'

'The discussion is closed, Rana. I don't want to hear any more. Go and change so you can help me here.'

In frustrated silence Rana left the room and went upstairs, too upset and angry to think coherently. She shut the bedroom door behind her and with suppressed violence pulled her suitcase out of the cupboard. Jeans, slacks, sweaters, a dress, nightclothes ... she piled them in haphazardly, her mind in a turmoil. She added rubber boots and a rain slicker, snapped the case shut and checked her watch. Heath should be here in about ten minutes. She hesitated irresolutely before throwing a light spring coat over her arm and opening the door. Then from downstairs she heard the sound of voices ...

Dorothea's and Eli's. With a lift of her heart, she knew an ally had arrived.

When she entered the lounge, her mother was standing by the Sheraton desk, her fingers tapping an angry tattoo on its polished surface; her face was mottled with temper.

'Well, Rana,' Eli drawled, 'it hasn't taken you long to get into hot water.'

She dropped a kiss on his wrinkled cheek, encouraged by the twinkle in his eye. 'Hello, Grandpa. I'm sorry I didn't see you at lunch time.'

'As I'm the one who sent Heath in my place, I seem to be at least partly responsible for this mix-up.' He eyed her keenly. 'Are you sure you want to go to Clearwater, Rana?'

She met his gaze squarely, smothering all the doubts and fears which had been plaguing her since Heath's invitation. 'Yes . . . yes, I do.'

He nodded slowly, then walked over to his daughter-in-law. 'Sit down a minute, Dorothea, and let me give you some fatherly advice.' He paused, gathering his thoughts. 'You'll regret it if you stop the child from going this weekend; you'll have nothing but trouble if you lay down the law. So let her go, Dorothea, and let her get it out of her system. It's by far the most sensible course of action. Rana's always been a good daughter to you—trust her now to do the right thing, why don't you?'

'I knew you'd be on her side,' Dorothea snapped, but even so, Rana could see she was somewhat mollified; her mother had always respected Eli's judgement.

'I'm on your side too,' Eli said gently.

Grudgingly Dorothea conceded, 'Well then, I suppose you'd better go, Rana. I'm sure I don't know how I'll explain it to Boyd.'

'I'll look after that,' Eli said in a voice that brooked no argument. 'You've done the right thing, Dorothea. Children can't be caged up—give Rana her freedom now and she'll come back to you.' His wise old face crinkled into a smile.

The doorbell chimed. Eli said, 'Is that Heath? Bring him in, Rana.'

Feeling ridiculously nervous, and hoping it didn't show, Rana swung open the big front door. Heath was standing there, the sun glinting in his wheat-gold hair, a faint smile on lips. Without preamble he asked, 'Did you survive the battle?'

She grinned ruefully. 'Well, yes—just. Eli came to my rescue in the nick of time.'

He threw back his head and laughed and she couldn't help joining him. 'Good girl!' he congratulated her. 'I knew you'd come through.'

'I almost didn't,' she confessed.

As he rested his hands on her shoulders, her body tingled from the contact. 'Next time I'll buy you a roomful of red roses—you've earned them.'

His praise made her blush with pleasure. 'Won't you come in?' she stammered. 'My things are in the hall.'

She preceded him into the living room, where immediately he went over to Dorothea. 'Mrs Liscombe, it's very kind of you to allow me to take Rana to Clearwater,' he said charmingly. 'I promise I'll take good care of her. We'll be back before dark on Sunday.' He turned to Rana's grandfather. 'Thanks, Eli,' he said, without specifying the source of his gratitude. The two men exchanged a masculine handshake of perfect understanding. 'Ready, Rana?' Heath continued. 'Is that your case?'

She nodded and gave Dorothea a kiss on the cheek. 'I'll see you on Sunday, Mother—thanks. 'Bye, Grandpa.' And then she and Heath were outdoors and he was stowing her suitcase in the trunk of his car. As they drove away, she knew in her bones that whatever happened this weekend, her life would never be the same again.

CHAPTER THREE

THE Cherokee taxied to a halt by the control tower, and Rana expelled her breath in a little sigh. 'That was fun!' she said spontaneously. 'I've never flown in a small plane before—there's really no comparison with one of the transatlantic jets, is there?'

Heath made a quick check of the instrument panel and turned off the ignition. 'Not really. I enjoy flying, I suppose because I'm a loner. It's certainly one way of getting away from it all!'

After he had checked in at the control tower, they walked across the grass to his jeep, parked by a rather dilapidated hangar. A fresh wind was blowing, moulding Rana's skirt against her legs and tugging at her hair; she was all too conscious of her companion's amusement as she tried to keep her hem more or less around her knees.

'I should have warned you to wear slacks, I guess,' he grinned, 'but I'm just as glad you didn't.'

She pulled a rude face at him as she clambered into the jeep with undignified haste. The tiny airport was on the outskirts of the town of Rexton, which consisted of an untidy cluster of wooden houses and small business establishments along a strip of paved road; the road itself abruptly ended at the town's limits. The sun glinted on the slow-moving waters that meandered into the forest.

'Beyond the river—that's the way to Clearwater,' Heath remarked, indicating the dirt track that led into the forest. 'Fifteen miles to home. But I guess we'd better pick up a few groceries first—come on.'

She followed him into a dimly lit clapboard store, piled high with every imaginable thing that one could need, she thought dazedly: canned goods, tools, clothing, fuel, feed, seeds ... nails in barrels, scythes hanging from the ceiling, boots scattered in one corner. From the top of a crumpled heap of potato sacks, a fat angora cat surveyed her superciliously.

'Rana, this is Jim Burden,' she heard Heath say. She shook hands with the towering, black-bearded figure who presided over this emporium. His smile was friendly enough as he rumbled a greeting, shifting the stub of a rank cigar from the corner of his mouth to do so.

From various unlikely places in the store Jim produced salad ingredients, fresh vegetables and neatly trimmed T-bone steaks. Heath added kerosene and a length of fishing line. 'What's been going on lately?' he enquired of the other man.

'Not much. Dance tomorrow night here in Rexton,' said Jim laconically. 'Pete's callin' and Vic and Curtis fiddlin'. Should be a good time. The two of you oughta come.'

'We just might. How much do I owe you?'

They piled their purchases in the back of the jeep and Heath said unnecessarily, 'We're off.' He grinned boyishly, revealing a more carefree side to his nature than she had seen before. 'I get as excited as a kid when I get this far, girl.'

She could not help being caught up in his anticipation and looked about her eagerly as they left Rexton for the narrow road into the wilderness. Tall spruce and fir, their limbs festooned with lichen, crowded to the very edge of the ditches, which were running with muddy water. Braken grew waist-high on the forest floor, their fronds, waving in the wind. The road itself deteriorated rapidly, its surface pitted with potholes and roughened by rocks sticking up from the ground.

'After a heavy rain, this is almost impassable,' Heath remarked. 'You're in mud up to the axles. But it's not too bad right now. Of course it freezes in winter; I have a truck equipped with a snowplough.' He ground to a halt so abruptly that Rana nearly fell off her seat. 'Look! Elk—see them?'

She glimpsed two heavy-set brown animals, one with a magnificent set of antlers, loping into the woods. 'You see a lot of them around Clearwater. They're no problem now, but beware a rutting bull in the fall—he can be a thoroughly unpredictable and bad-tempered beast.' As they continued on their way, he showed her partridge scratching in the gravel and rabbits skittering off into the bush, and patiently answered all her questions about the wild life, questions which revealed her abysmal ignorance. In no time, or so it seemed to Rana, they rounded one last corner and emerged into a clearing. Heath stopped the jeep and helped her out. In silence she looked around her.

They were standing on a slight rise. Grassy slopes, dotted with wild strawberry blooms, stretched in front of them to the shores of the lake. On her left, built into a hollow in the ground and sheltered by pines, was the main house, solidly constructed of rounded logs with a slate roof and huge stone chimneys at either end; a wide verandah flanked three sides. The windows, reflecting the rays of the sun, twinkled a welcome. For all its size, the house was not pretentious; it promised shelter and comfort, she thought, her eyes wandering over its simple lines and warmly burnished wood. Not far from the house a wharf had been built out into the lake. Hills rose from the far shore, their rounded, tree-clad bulk majestic against the sky. Whitecaps ruffled the surface of the lake and wavelets slapped rhythmically at the jetty, while the wind sighed through the forest. Piercingly sweet, a bird's song rippled from a stand of silver birches.

'A hermit thrush. A pair of them nest here every year,' Heath said quietly. 'What do you think of the place?'

'It's so vast and wild and incredibly beautiful.' She hesitated, afraid he would laugh at her. 'This sounds silly, I suppose—but it makes me want to sing and dance and shout.'

'I know exactly what you mean,' he chuckled. 'I don't tell everyone this, but more than once I've stood in this very spot and howled at the moon! And from the far hills heard the wolves cry back.'

'You mean there are wolves?' She was unable to suppress a shiver.

'Oh, yes—don't forget we're a long way from civilisation here.' He added prosaically, 'I'll drive the jeep down to the house and we'll unpack.'

When they walked up the verandah steps to the front door, they discovered a note tacked to the panels. Heath ripped it open and remarked casually, 'It's from Polly, my housekeeper. She's gone to visit her family at Smoky River. She won't be back until next week. Guess we'll have to fend for ourselves—hope you're a good cook!'

'You mean there's nobody here but us?' Rana asked in dismay.

'That's right.' He unlocked the door and picked up their cases.

She put a staying hand on his arm. 'But I can't stay here alone with you.'

'Why ever not?'

She gazed at him helplessly. 'It's just not done.'

'Rana, let's get one thing straight. This isn't your mother's house in Edmonton. This is Clearwater. And in Clearwater we live by a different set of rules—my rules. As far as I'm concerned it doesn't matter in the slightest whether Polly is here or not.'

'You knew she'd be gone!'

'Don't be silly,' he retorted wearily, 'it didn't even occur to me to wonder about her whereabouts. If it's your precious virtue you're worrying about, allow me to tell you something—if I wanted to seduce you, I'd do it if there were fifty people here. Now will you quit being so damned uptight and help me with this stuff?'

Rana bit her lip in vexation, picked up the bag of groceries and stepped over the threshold, walking almost immediately into the large living room, its picture windows overlooking the choppy waters of the lake. A stone fireplace took up the far wall, with built-in bookshelves on either side of it; the other walls were panelled in pale knotty pine. A huge Persian rug, intricately patterned in reds and blues, lay on the hardwood floor. The comfortable armchairs and chesterfield were upholstered in deep red velvet, multicoloured cushions scattered on them in pleasant disarray.

Forgetting their altercation, for she was not a girl to sulk, she exclaimed, 'What a lovely room!'

'Thanks. We'll light a fire after supper. The evenings can be cool here. The kitchen's through this way, Rana—do you want to bring the groceries?'

The kitchen, although decorated with rustic simplicity, nevertheless had every modern convenience, Rana was quick to notice. Bright gingham curtains hung at the windows and copper pans dangled from the oak-beamed ceiling, along with bunches of dried herbs. As in the living room, she saw oil lamps resting in niches in the wall.

'They're for emergencies,' Heath explained. 'I have my own generator for electricity, but it's just as well not to be totally dependent on that. Dump that stuff and I'll show you your room.'

Her bedroom at the back of the house had wall-to-wall moss green carpeting and furniture of darkly stained cherry; the bedspread and matching drapes were made of daintily flowered chintz. 'Your house is beautiful, Heath,' Rana said in genuine appreciation. 'You must have had a struggle getting some of these things up here!'

'It wasn't easy,' he agreed. 'Listen, before we start to cook supper, let's walk down to the lake. I need to stretch my legs.'

'Sure.'

Together they strolled down the slope to the shore. Rana breathed deeply, filling her lungs with the mingled scents of lake water and pine needles and wet turf, all carried to her on the boisterous wind.

'Glad you came?' Heath asked. She nodded shyly. 'Then I'm going to do something I've wanted to do ever since I first saw you.'

She stood quite still, a mute question in her face. He reached out and swiftly pulled the pins from her hair, so that in a silken swathe it tumbled to her shoulders, where the wind seized it and playfully tangled it around her neck. 'You have beautiful hair, Rana,' he said, stroking a pale tendril back from her forehead. 'When you're with me, will you wear it loose?'

It never occurred to her to refuse. 'Yes, of course,' she said simply.

He put his arm around her shoulders and sought her lips in a kiss of such tenderness that unconsciously her body swayed towards his. He raised his head and said softly, 'Welcome to Clearwater, Rana.'

In perfect accord they smiled at each other, his face so close to hers that she could see the tiny flecks of rust in the smoke grey of his eyes. Then he said in deliberate withdrawal, 'Well, this isn't getting supper on the table, is it?' His manner was so down to earth that Rana wondered if she had imagined the brief intimacy they had shared.

Swallowing a strange sense of disappointment, she said brightly, 'It seems a long time since we had lunch.'

They ate a delicious meal of broiled steak, tossed salad, and homemade rolls which Heath had taken out of the freezer; sitting at the kitchen table, which overlooked the water, they watched the sun set in orange splendour at the head of the lake, and the first star shimmer in the sky. From behind the hills came a pale radiance heralding the rising moon. The wind had dropped, and gradually the lake smoothed to a sheet of obsidian. Rana was so captivated by the beauty of the scene that she gave a start when Heath said, 'Let's wash the dishes and go canoeing . . . it's a perfect night for it.'

With alacrity she got to her feet and began piling the dirty plates in the sink, stopping only to roll up the sleeves of her white blouse. Heath handed her the coffee mugs, and as she took them from him, he exclaimed, 'What happened there?'

'Where?' she asked in puzzlement.

'Your wrists.'

She glanced down and blushed in confusion, trying to hide the blotched purple bruises with her other hand. 'It must have happened last night, when you were holding on to me,' she stammered. 'I bruise easily—I always have.'

'I did that to you?'

'Well—yes.'

'God! I'm sorry.' He encircled her wrists in his big hands, his touch exquisitely gentle, and raised them to his mouth, caressing her soft skin with his lips so that she trembled with delight. Greatly daring, she leaned forward and rested her cheek on his bent head, her face buried in his thick hair. His tongue probed her flesh and then he said, his voice muffled, 'The pulse in your wrist is beating like a trip-hammer.' He looked up. 'It excites you when I touch you, doesn't it, Rana?'

'How can I deny it?' she said ruefully.

'Don't try—just enjoy it, girl.'

A gush of water came from the sink and unceremoniously Heath dropped her hands. 'Hell! We left the tap running!' He dashed over and turned it off and the spell between them was broken. Not talking much, which in Rana's case at least was because she did not know what to say, they washed and dried the dishes. After they had finished, Heath asked, 'Did you bring your jeans? Wear them, and bring a jacket. I'll meet you down at the wharf in a few minutes.'

When she ventured outside, the moon was fully visible, a perfect silver circle in the sky, throwing its beams in a narrow path on the still black waters of the lake. There was not a breath of wind; the silence was so complete it seemed to have an existence of its own.

The screech of a wooden door shattered the quiet. On her left she saw Heath emerge from a wooden shed, bearing the canoe on his back. She walked to meet him. He was wearing a woollen checked shirt and corduroy trousers, with laced-up leather boots; in coming to Clearwater he seemed to have shed some of the veneer of civilisation, for he looked tough and resourceful and completely at home in this untamed world. His boots rattled on the stones as he lowered the canoe into the lake, its prow slapping the surface into spreading ripples.

'Have you ever paddled a canoe before?' he asked. She shook her head. 'But you can swim?'

'Oh, yes,' she replied, glad she could answer in the affirmative for once.

'Okay. I'll put you in the bow. You hold the paddle like this—one hand here and the other down here. Take slow, regular strokes. Try not to scrape the side—that's hard on the canoe and on your fingers!'

As she stepped into the craft, it wobbled dangerously and she clutched the sides to keep her balance.

'Walk exactly down the middle and crouch low ... canoes are temperamental,' Heath instructed. After she had reached the seat without further mishap, and picked up the paddle, Heath pushed off and they glided away from the jetty. For the first few minutes Rana was totally occupied with the mechanics of paddling, but gradually she acquired the slow, easy rhythm that was needed, and was able to look around her.

Heath was steadily steering them towards a cluster of tiny islands that rose black out of the water at the western end of the lake. The sky behind them was studded with a myriad of stars, all seemingly so much brighter here than in the city; the girl was overwhelmed by the sense of mystery and vast distance that they covered. From the hills came the eerie hoting of an owl. The only other sound was the splash and gurgle of the paddles.

As they approached the largest island, Heath said

quietly, 'I'll beach the canoe between those rocks. Can you jump out on shore and tie the hawser round a tree trunk?'

With a jolt the canoe hit bottom. Rana stood up and jumped for the shore, but at the last minute the canoe shifted under her, and she miscalculated the distance, landing up to her knees in cold water. She gave a little shriek of shock. 'Ouch! It's freezing!'

From his perch in the stern Heath laughed heartlessly. 'I said to tie up the canoe, girl, not go for a swim!'

She glared at him, and with sudden inspiration hit the water with the flat of her paddle, so that he was doused in a shower of spray. 'Come on in,' she said sweetly. 'The water's fine.'

She should have known better. In three swift strokes he backed the canoe away from the island, until he was well out of her reach. 'How are you going to get home, Rana?' he taunted. 'Swim?'

'Heath Markland, come back here!'

'Why? After all, the water's fine, you said so yourself.'

She scrambled up on the rocks, giggling helplessly. From behind her there came a loud rustling and scratching in the undergrowth. 'Heath, what's that?' she screeched.

'It's probably only a bear. I hope you didn't wake him up—they don't like that.'

She stood stock still, torn between laughter and fright. The moon cast strange shadows over the island, distorting the tree branches into clutching fingers, making menacing, hump-backed creatures out of the heaped grey boulders. Then, almost at her feet, a dark shape heaved itself up from the ground, and in genuine panic she retreated to the water's edge. Forgetting her pride, she pleaded, 'Heath, come and get me. There's something there.'

He brought the canoe in and joined her on the shore, looping the painter over a stump. She clutched at him, his warm bulk infinitely comforting. 'It was a big animal over there in the rocks,' she quavered. 'I nearly stepped on it.'

He hugged her briefly, and went to investigate, poking among the boulders with a stick. There was a scrabbling and a splash, and she saw a V-shaped furrow appear as the creature swam away. 'Only a beaver,' Heath said dryly.

'It looked bigger than a beaver,' she said defensively, feeling rather ridiculous about the fuss she had made.

'Perhaps it was a big one,' he replied in amusement. 'We'd better head back, Rana. I don't want you to get cold.'

When they reached the jetty, Heath anchored the canoe and they walked up the slope to the house. He had left a light burning in the kitchen; its yellow glow beamed a brave welcome against the backdrop of tall trees. 'You'd better get out of your wet clothes,' he suggested. 'Put on something more comfortable and join me for a nightcap by the fire, why don't you?'

She had a quick shower and brushed her hair until it shone. After some hesitation she donned a peacock blue caftan of silky brocade, its heavy folds subtly emphasising the slender lines of her figure. Her bare feet soundless on the board floors, she padded into the living room. The only light was cast by the crackling flames in the fireplace; Heath was just adding another log. When he straightened and turned, he caught sight of her and for an instant his body was frozen to a hunter's stillness. The firelight flickered over the fabric of her gown, its barbaric sheen enhancing the brilliant blue of her eyes; her hair fell down her back in a pale sheaf. She shifted under his relentless scrutiny, a flush delineating her cheekbones, and said finally, 'Is anything wrong?'

'The only thing wrong is that you're far too desirable for my peace of mind.'

He put down the log and walked over to her. He too had changed from his canoeing clothes, she noticed, into dark velvet trousers and a pale blue shirt, every detail of his appearance burned into her brain as she waited. Keeping his arms at his sides, he lowered his head and began kissing her, his lips moving insistently against hers, drinking deep of the sweetness of her mouth. In spite of herself, her arms crept around his neck, until she was suddenly seized and crushed to his lean body. She could feel the muscles of his thighs, the hardness of his chest, the sinewy strength of his encircling arms; her nerve endings quivered with desire. Slowly he gentled the searching pressure of his mouth, burying his face in her neck to inhale the sweet scent of her hair. When finally he looked up, her lustrous eyes blazed with the passion he had evoked.

His voice was totally under control when he spoke. 'Beautiful Rana ... come by the fire and I'll put some music on.' Her knees weak, she sank down on the bearskin rug by the hearth, propping one elbow on the cushions piled there. The lilting melody of a Mozart sonata drifted across the room from the magnificent stereo equipment beside a shelf of records and tapes—another facet of this complex man was plainly a love of good music.

He joined her by the fire and handed her a glass of creamy liquid sprinkled with nutmeg. 'Brandy Alexander. I hope you like it.'

She sipped it slowly, needing time to recover her equilibrium; he, she couldn't help noticing, seemed totally divorced from their lovemaking of a few minutes ago, and was staring pensively into the flames. But then he glanced up and she saw slumbrous desire in the grey depths of his eyes, and knew he had not forgotten. 'Do you listen to much music?' she asked at random.

'Yes—especially when I'm here alone. My tastes are quite catholic, from Bach to the Beatles! What about you?'

They embarked on an animated discussion of their favourites. Thoroughly enjoying herself, Rana sat up cross-legged, tucking her long robe around her feet and leaning forward to emphasise what she was saying, her face lit by a lively intelligence. A loop of hair fell across her shoulder. She pushed it back impatiently, gesturing with her hands as she always did when she was excited. Heath laughed at something she said. She smiled at him unselfconsciously, all her nervousness about the week-end dissipated in the joy of a new-found companionship. 'You're fun to be with!' she said spontaneously.

'So are you. Nevertheless, if we're going to be up at five a.m. to catch a trout for breakfast'—he grinned as she winced theatrically—'we should get to bed fairly soon.'

'If you go out and catch them, I'll cook them for you,' she offered. 'At a more civilised hour like eight o'clock, that is.'

'Oh no . . . this is the age of sexual equality, hadn't you heard? We both get up at five.'

She finished her drink and stretched sinuously. 'I hope you have an alarm clock.'

'I'll wake up—don't you worry. And I'll wake you up too.'

'Thanks a lot! I'll see you in the morning, then.'

About to leave, she halted when he said, 'Come here, Rana.' Shyly she edged closer to the cushions on which he was half reclining. 'You must kiss me goodnight be-fore you go.'

Without a trace of coyness she knelt beside him and leaned over to kiss him, steadying herself with her hand against his chest. As their lips met, she could feel the heavy thud of his heart beneath her palm, and this tang-ible evidence that she was arousing him spread a glow of warmth through her limbs.

His arms came around her, pulling her on top of him, even as his lips moved against hers with ever-increasing force. One hand became entangled in her hair, the other smoothed the curve of her spine, caressing her hips and pressing her closer to his lean length. His mouth nuzzled the slenderness of her throat. He murmured, 'Your skin is so incredibly soft.'

She gave a little sigh of pure delight as she stroked the hair back from his forehead, dropping tiny kisses on his face, as she sought to memorise every inch of his features. Dimly she became aware that, lying as she was, the neck of her caftan had fallen open, exposing the deep valley between her breasts to his view. He pushed the thick brocade to one side, nibbling the soft swell of her flesh, until she moaned with pleasure. Of their own accord her fingers fumbled with the buttons of his shirt, baring the broad expanse of his chest.

'Rana,' he said huskily, 'I want you.' In one lithe movement he pulled her to her feet, then gathered her in his arms, holding her as though she was infinitely precious. His penetrating eyes explored her flushed cheeks and the agitated rise and fall of her bosom. 'Come with me.'

Bemused as she was, it took her a minute to realise he was carrying her to his bedroom. As he pushed open the door, her body tensed in his arms. He laid her on the bed and began peeling off his shirt, his broad shoulders and muscled torso somehow menacing in the gloom.

'Heath——' she whispered, 'no——'

'What's wrong?' he asked tenderly.

'I've never—made love before. I can't——'

'I understand, Rana. I'll be gentle with you.'

'You don't understand!' she contradicted, lifting her hands in an eloquent plea for sympathy. 'I can't make love to you, Heath.'

'Why not?' There was a thin thread of implacable anger in his voice.

Distraught, knowing she was not explaining herself well, she stammered, 'I've only just met you, and——'

'That has nothing to do with it, girl, you know that as well as I do. When two people strike sparks from each other as we do, it's an instant reaction. The chemistry's right, and believe me, you're crazy not to take advantage of it.'

The white fire he had kindled in her body cried out that he was right. She smothered it fiercely, and gathering her courage, blurted, 'We can't go to bed together—I'm not married to you!'

There was an instant's deadly silence. 'I should have known you'd drag out your puritanical morality!' he said grimly.

She took refuge in anger. 'You know damn well if I said yes, you'd think I was cheap—just another easy woman.'

'I'd think you had the courage and warmth to do what you want to do.'

'Do what you want! Take whatever's offered! So that's your morality,' she retorted bitterly. 'I'll stick with mine, thank you.'

'Then you'd better marry Boyd. The two of you are well suited.'

Cut to the quick, she still made one last bid for understanding, steadying her voice with an effort. 'Heath,' she said quietly, 'we're talking about making love—and that's the whole point, that second word ... love. It implies caring and commitment. Otherwise how are we different from animals?'

He laughed cynically. 'The classic female argument!'

'And you're the classic male—frightened of feelings, scared to admit real emotion.'

'Don't push me too far, Rana,' he warned. 'My patience isn't inexhaustible.'

She got to her feet, her silk gown swishing in heavy folds to the ground. He flicked it contemptuously. 'And next time, don't wear something as seductive as this—I loathe false pretences.'

Flinching as though he had struck her, she fought back tears of mingled pain and rage.

'Go to bed, Rana ... your own bed. I'll see you in the morning.' He turned his back on her in clear dismissal.

On soundless feet she ran to her room and shut the door behind her. Pulling the caftan over her head, she flung it in a heap on the floor, vowing never to wear it again. She put on a white nightgown and crept into bed, the sheets cool on her fevered skin. For a long time she lay staring into the blackness, until finally by forcefully blotting out the memory of their ugly confrontation, she was able to sleep ...

CHAPTER FOUR

SOMEONE was shaking her by the shoulder. Twisting away, she burrowed her head deeper in the pillows.

'Rana! Wake up.'

As her consciousness struggled to the surface, she realised it was Heath, and the memory of the disastrous scene in his bedroom flooded over her again. Still keeping her face hidden, she mumbled something unintelligible, wanting only to sink back into the oblivion of sleep. But his fingers remained clamped on her shoulder. 'Wake up,' he repeated.

There was genuine amusement in his voice. Perhaps it was this that gave her the courage to turn over; she blinked at him drowsily in the dim dawn light. He was already dressed, in the clothes he had worn for canoeing. 'What time is it?' she asked.

'Time to get up.'

'I only just went to bed.'

'Nonsense—you've had at least six hours' sleep.'

'I can't stand people who are full of sweetness and light first thing in the morning,' she grumbled, half sitting up in bed to see what her watch said, the sheets inadvertently slipping to her waist. 'It's only five o'clock!' she exclaimed, grimacing at him in horror.

But he did not notice. His eyes were devouring her tumbled hair and bare shoulders, and the pale curve of her breast glimmering through the filmy nylon nightdress. He said lazily, 'If you really don't want to get up, we could always stay here.'

Colour rose in her cheeks, and she grabbed at the sheet. But he stayed her hand, grinning at her confusion, and for a minute they engaged in an undignified tug of war. Laughing, she said, 'Heath——'

'Women!' he groaned theatrically. 'They'll do anything to keep a man from going fishing.'

Wide awake now, she said indignantly, 'if you'd go away, I could get dressed. I hope my breakfast's ready?'

'I can take a hint. You've got five minutes.'

As he left the room and Rana hurriedly scrambled out of bed, she could not help marvelling at his radical changes of mood—his cruel anger of last night, as contrasted with his lighthearted raillery of a few minutes ago. How was she to understand him?

As the day progressed, she came no nearer to solving the problem. They went fishing in the canoe and she experienced the thrill of a strike and the excitement of hauling in a twelve-inch speckled trout. Heath cooked their catch for lunch, frying the thick pink fillets in lemon butter; Rana had never tasted anything so delicious in her life. They spent the afternoon in the living room, she reading and listening to music, he working on some accounts for his business. And for the evening he had suggested a trip into Rexton to the square dance.

Yet all day, although on one level she was enjoying herself, delighted by the novelty of so many new experiences, she also had the baffling sensation that he had retreated somewhere beyond her reach, hiding himself behind a barrier of good-natured camaraderie; she might have been his younger sister for all the attention he showed her as a woman. He was friendly and good company: she certainly could not complain on that score. So what was wrong?

She deplored her own lack of logic, for last night she had been the one to back away from the searing heat of their mutual desire; so now, she should have been pleased that he was making no attempt to touch her or kiss her ... it should have been a relief to find his manner so impersonal. Yet, with her innate honesty, she had to admit that his continued withdrawal both hurt and bewildered her, and as the day slowly passed, her body began to clamour for the touch of his hands, for the assurance that he found her desirable. But her pride would not allow her to acknowledge this need to him.

Increasingly she wondered if she had ruined something precious. Had she destroyed the unique closeness they had shared by her shyness, her fear, her 'middle class morality'? She was appalled by the abyss that this prospect opened before her. The intensity of her regret startled and frightened her. How, in so short a time, had Heath Markland made such inroads into her closely guarded inner life? It was as though he had aroused her to the infinite possibilities of passion between man and woman, and had then turned his back on her, leaving her unable to retreat into her previously cloistered existence, yet unable to cope with her newly awakened desires. She grew more silent and tense as evening deepened over Clearwater, although Heath did not appear to notice any change in her. She was almost glad when it was time to leave for the dance—at least they would meet other people in Rexton, and escape from the isolation of looming hills and silent lake.

Heath parked the jeep in a row of other cars and trucks and glanced at his companion. 'Ever been to a square dance?'

'I learned some of the steps years ago in school, but I'm sure I've forgotten them all by now.' She smiled at him uncertainly. He was wearing an open-necked shirt and slim-hipped jeans, and looked relaxed and comfortable. After some thought, she herself had put on a flounced cotton skirt and a pale blue blouse of broderie anglaise, with thin-strapped sandals on her feet.

They left the jeep and she gazed around her, wide-eyed. A wooden platform, some two feet off the ground, held the dancers and fiddlers; clustered lights on tall poles shed light on the swirling patterns of the sets. The backdrop was the inky blackness of the sky, all the stars obscured by clouds. The two fiddlers were playing an Irish jig, while the caller cried, 'Bow to your partner and a do-se-do ... opposite corners and allemand ...' And reverberating over everything was the thud-thud of the men's boots on the board floor and the whoops and clapping of the spectators.

Rana, suddenly shy, would have hung back, but Heath grabbed her by the hand and pulled her up the steps behind him, and in no time they were part of a set. For a few minutes she stumbled uncertainly through the intricate movements. But then it all fell into place; she twirled and curtseyed and stamped her feet and was heartily sorry when the music ended with a flourish. Heath came back over to her, another couple with him.

'Rana, I'd like you to meet some good friends of mine, Beth and Jim Hinton. Jim's the local doctor. Most of his patients manage to survive him!'

Jim aimed a mock blow in Heath's direction and smiled at Rana in open approval. 'Hi, Rana!' He was a stocky, dark-haired man in his early thirties, laughter wrinkles around his kind brown eyes; instinctively Rana was sure he could be trusted implicitly. His wife Beth was a small, plump woman with a head of ruffled, copper-coloured curls, and a vivacious smile; she was holding hands with her husband, whom she plainly adored. For a few minutes the two couples chatted together, but then the fiddlers tuned up and a vigorous Virginia reel got under way.

Soon Rana's cheeks were flushed with exertion and her eyes bright with pleasure. She could not help contrasting this uninhibited outdoor celebration with some of her her mother's sedate gatherings—how much she preferred this one! Somehow she and Heath became separated; she polkaed with burly lumbermen and waltzed with cowboys from the ranches south of Rexton, occasionally able to flash a smile at him across the width of the platform.

During the entire evening there was only one sour note—one of Heath's lumberjacks, Bill Stewart by name, was her partner for a waltz, and it was not until they had begun dancing that Rana realised he had had far too much to drink. He held her unpleasantly close and although his conversation was innocuous enough there was an insolent and suggestive undertone. She was glad when Heath cut in and finished the dance with her.

It came as a distinct shock to feel a raindrop hit her cheek, and then another and another. With the suddenness of a cloudburst the heavens opened and the rain descended in a deluge. Heath seized her elbow. 'Run for the jeep!'

They fled from the platform and raced to their vehicle, Rana leaping into her seat with the agility of a deer. She slammed the door, tucking her wet hair behind her ears. Her blouse was moulded to her figure and her skirt to her thighs; her sandals would never be the same again. Heath was equally damp. 'Well, that ends that!' he said ruefully. 'Did you enjoy yourself?'

'Oh yes! I had a marvellous time. Thanks for taking me.'

'My pleasure. And now we'd better head home fast or we'll be in trouble. The creek at the boundary of the Clearwater property floods every time there's a heavy rain. But with any luck we'll get there before it gets too deep.'

They drove almost in silence, for Rana sensed Heath needed all his concentration for the road. The rain came down in sheets, distorting his vision in spite of the windshield wipers. Water ran in rivulets along the track, while at times the wheels slewed sideways in the grip of thick, glue-like mud. Rana clutched the edges of her seat, shivering with cold from her damp garments. She had confidence in Heath's ability to handle the jeep, but even so, was awestruck by the rapidity with which the elements could transform an ordinary dirt road into a treacherous quagmire.

After some ten or eleven miles Heath said grimly, not taking his eyes from the road, 'We should have stayed in Rexton—the Hintons would have put us up. I didn't think it would get this bad so quickly.'

The rear of the jeep skidded sharply and he swung the wheel, muttering an oath under his breath. But he was not fast enough. One of the back wheels began to spin in the slippery mud, so that the jeep lurched sideways into the ditch.

Heath straightened the steering, then tried alternating between first gear and reverse, rocking the vehicle to get it back on the road. 'Damnation!' he grunted finally. 'Rana, you'll have to drive. I'll get out and push. If it goes ahead, don't stop until you're back in the middle of the road.'

She slid into his seat, first rolling down the window so she could hear his shouted instructions. 'Ready!' he yelled.

She eased the lever into first gear and cautiously pressed on the accelerator. The wheel spun viciously, but for a few seconds the jeep inched forward. 'Again!' came Heath's voice out of the darkness.

On her third attempt there was enough traction for her to regain the road. She stopped the jeep, and with a sigh of relief surrendered the driver's seat to Heath, whose shirt was now plastered to his body and whose hands were grimed with dirt. 'Thanks—you did a good job,' he said, his casual words of praise instilling in her a glow of pleasure. 'Not far now to the creek; I hope we can get across. If not, we'll be between the devil and the deep blue sea—it sure as hell wouldn't be safe to drive back to Rexton with the road in this condition.'

Up until now, Rana had not been particularly frightened, but hearing Heath admit that he was worried, was enough to erode her confidence. Then the twin beams of the headlights flashed upon the creek. Rana gasped. From a quiet trickle of water that normally ran under the road in a wide metal pipe, it had turned into a raging torrent mixed with branches and tumbling rocks; it had flooded the road in at least two feet of water.

Heath slammed on the brakes. 'Well, that's that,' he said heavily. 'Sorry, Rana, I should have had better sense.' He rolled down his window and peered out into the night. 'The rain's letting up a bit, I think. The creek'll probably have gone down enough by morning so that we can get across. In the meantime I guess we stay put.'

'Oh,' she said blankly. 'You mean we just stay here?'

'That's exactly what I mean. We could perhaps wade across the creek, but then we're still three miles from home—and you're not exactly dressed for walking.'

She glanced down at her ruined sandals. 'You are so right.'

'It's okay. I always carry a bedroll and some emergency supplies in the jeep.'

A frisson rippled along her spine. Her eyes huge, she nervously pleated the fabric of her skirt in her fingers. She was being given no choice: she would have to spend the night with Heath in the cramped quarters of the jeep. In silence she watched as he unfolded three heavy blankets and spread them out in the back.

'It probably won't be very comfortable,' he said matter-of-factly. 'But it's a hell of a lot better than being out in the rain. I've spent more than one night in the bush in a rainstorm—no fun, I can assure you.'

Gratefully she sensed that he was aware of her tension, and was talking to relax her. He held out his hand. 'Here, climb between the seats.'

She laid her hand in his and clambered awkwardly into the back, half kneeling on the blankets to avoid bumping her head on the roof. He exclaimed, 'Your hand's like ice!' chafing her fingers in his far warmer ones. She smiled weakly, for she had been trying to subdue her shivers ever since they left Rexton. He touched the damp material of her blouse where it clung to her shoulders. 'You're soaking.' He hesitated. 'Look, Rana,' he said flatly, 'this is no time for false modesty. You'll catch pneumonia if you stay in those wet things. Take them off—don't look so shocked, I'll turn my back—and get under the blankets.'

She opened her mouth to argue but closed it again, sensible enough to know that what he suggested was the only practical course of action. She *was* cold, chilled to the bone, and was longing to get out of her wet clothes. He turned away, and she pulled the blouse over her head and then clumsily eased out of her skirt, hanging them both over the back of her seat. The blankets were rough on her skin as she huddled under them, curling her knees up for warmth.

He shrugged off his shirt, pushing his wet hair back from his forehead in an impatient gesture that already she recognised as characteristic of him. Then he too slid under the blankets, carefully not touching her. 'Try and go to sleep,' he murmured.

'Goodnight.' Rana lay as still as she could, listening to the rain drumming on the roof. The wind had come up, whipping the tree branches into a frenzy. She tried to imagine how she would feel if she were alone here, and gave a little shudder, unconsciously hunching closer to Heath. Resolutely she closed her eyes. But sleep evaded her. She was still cold, and much as she tried, she could not control the spasms of shivering that shook her frame.

'Rana, are you warm now?'

She hesitated too long. His hand reached out to her bare shoulder, immediately sensing her body's uncontrollable tremors. Before she realised his intension, he put his arms around her and pulled her closer to him, wincing as her cold hands met his flesh. 'God!' he exclaimed. 'If the old saying is right—cold hands, warm heart—you must be the most warm-hearted person I know!'

Reassured by his banter, she gave a little sigh and gradually relaxed against him, burrowing her face into his shoulder, her long hair falling across his arm. Warmth from his body seeped into hers, so that her shivering ceased. She felt utterly safe in the circle of his arms: safe from the raging of the storm, and the deep-seated, primitive fear of the night. Almost asleep, she muttered drowsily, 'You're nice to sleep with.'

'Thank you. So are you.' But she was asleep.

It was still dark when she awoke. For a moment she was frightened and disorientated by the strange surroundings, until she remembered the wild drive through the night and their enforced stay in the jeep. Heath was lying close beside her, one hand entangled in her hair. But he was thrashing restlessly in his sleep, and she realised that was why she had awakened. Suddenly he cried out, 'Craig! Craig—no!' his voice hoarse with such pain that for an instant Rana was frozen into immobility. Then instinctively she put her arms around him.

'Heath—wake up! You're having a nightmare.'

He twisted away from her, moaning something unintelligible. She shook him. 'Heath, please wake up,' she pleaded.

He gave a start. 'What's wrong? Rana—are you all right?'

'You were dreaming, it woke me.'

'Oh hell, I'm sorry. Did I —say anything?'

'Well, yes. You called out someone's name . . . Craig?'

He did not answer right away; she could feel him lying unnaturally still beside her.

'Who is Craig, Heath?'

'It's not a pretty story, Rana . . . there's no need for you to know about it. I'm only sorry I woke you. Try and go to sleep again.'

Her eyes were accustomed to the dark now. His face was so close to hers that she could see the deeply carved lines of strain around his mouth, and the depths of some unassuaged agony in his eyes. It seemed intolerable to her that he should bear whatever burden it was alone, so she said forthrightly, 'Please tell me—wouldn't it be better to share it?'

He buried his face in his arms. 'I don't know—I suppose it might.'

'Craig—was he your brother?' she asked in swift discernment, not even sure why she should say 'was', yet knowing Craig was dead.

'Yes, he was.' He turned over, reaching out for her as though drawing comfort from her nearness; she could feel his breath fanning her cheek.

'Tell me about him.'

'We were always close, Craig and I, ever since we were kids,' he began. 'I suppose losing our parents and then going to live with our grandfather in the cabin at Clearwater made a bond between us. There was hardly ever anyone else to play with, so we spent nearly all our time together.' A reminiscent smile softened his mouth. 'We had a tree house about a mile from the cabin ... cut all the lumber ourselves, bought nails with money we earned on a trapline, and built it, just the two of us. It became everything from a settlers' fort to a pirate ship, that tree house. We had some great times in it ...'

An indescribable sensation of happiness pervaded her, that he should share his memories with her. But all she said was, 'Didn't you go to school?'

'Oh, periodically Granddad would have fits of conscience and send us into Rexton for a few weeks. But we were to used to being free and untramelled to settle down at a desk, especially Craig. He always was a wanderer, as restless as the prairie wind. I guess we both must have been bright enough; we passed our matriculation exams with no trouble, in spite of our rather haphazard school career.'

'Then what did you do?' she asked, fascinated by these glimpses into Heath's past.

'I went off to the University of Toronto and Craig——'

'What did you study?'

'Commerce and business administration—that was no

trouble. But being in a city had its problems. I used to spend nearly every weekend in the fall and the spring canoeing in Algonquin Park!'

'And Craig?'

'He got his pilot's licence, bought a secondhand plane, and took off up north. No universities or cities for Craig. But he was shrewd enough to build up his own business in the next five years: ten planes, a flying doctor service to the Indians and Eskimos, a contract for supplying goods to air force bases. He never let himself be trapped behind a desk—he was always up in one of his planes, usually taking the most dangerous runs.'

There was a brief silence, and Rana guessed they were getting to the crux of the matter. Slowly Heath continued, 'When I graduated, I came back to Alberta, and Craig and I picked up where we left off. We'd fly to Vancouver or Calgary for weekends, and between us we'd paint the town red—we had some great times together. I started building the house at Clearwater, and every so often he'd land his seaplane on the lake—usually after seeing how close he could fly to the chimney tops!—help me for a day or two, then take off again. He never could stay long in one place. He had no Clearwater of his own, not Craig.'

'He must have been fun to be with, though?'

'He sure was. He was one of the most alive people I've ever met. I've often wondered if he knew subconsciously that he hadn't long to live. He always swore he'd die with his boots on . . .'

'And that's what happened?' she murmured gently, curling herself closer to Heath in an unspoken gesture of comfort. He patted her shoulder absently, his thoughts far away.

'He met a girl in Calgary, Cheryl was her name. She was beautiful and lively and intelligent, and was beginning to establish herself as a sculptor of some repute. They fell in love. Craig never did anything by half measures—it used to frighten me to see how completely he loved and trusted her.' He gave a brief, bitter laugh. 'Well, you can probably guess what happened. It was inevitable, I suppose. They got engaged—but he wanted to live up north and she wanted to live in Calgary. He wouldn't give up flying and his nomadic life, she wouldn't give up her career. They had one row after another ... and then finally in November she moved in with a friend of hers, a portrait painter who had just left his wife.'

'Oh, Heath, how dreadful! Whatever did Craig do?'

'He came to Clearwater, heading north for good, he said. He wanted me to go with him to deliver some building supplies to a newly established trading post near Great Slave Lake. It didn't take much persuasion—he looked desperate enough to fly into the nearest mountain. I couldn't let him go alone.'

Rana lay still in Heath's arms, every nerve alert to the gathering tension in his lean frame. His voice roughened. 'Late in the afternoon we picked up the stuff in Edmonton and took off. What happened is partly my fault: I assumed he'd checked the met. reports and logged his flight with the control tower—those are routine things no pilot ever neglects. But that day, Craig forgot them ... late at night we ran into bad weather, snow that changed to freezing rain. The wings iced up and we knew we'd have to land. But the visibility was almost nil and Craig miscalculated the distance. We slammed into the cliffs on the edge of a lake and the plane went through the ice.'

He shuddered. 'I'll never forget the next few minutes. Craig was unconscious, but somehow I got him out of the plane and up on to the ice. I dragged him to shore, and made a fire and some kind of a rough shelter. That was the longest night of my life. We hadn't been able to radio our position and nobody knew where we were. If the search planes did get out, they had thousands of square miles to cover. We didn't even have the plane as a marker; it had sunk without a trace.'

'What did you do?' she whispered, so caught up in his narrative that she could almost hear the keening north wind and feel the bite of ice pellets on her skin.

'I stayed put for three days, hoping against hope that help would come. While I waited, I built a sled and snared rabbits and looked after Craig—he was badly hurt. But there was no sign of another plane, and I finally decided my only hope was to go south in the general direction of Fort Vermilion, because if Craig didn't get medical attention soon, I knew he wouldn't survive. For three days I hauled him on that sled. Up and down hills, through muskeg, across the barrens. But he got steadily worse, and on the fourth day he lapsed into unconsciousness.'

His hands dug into her soft flesh and he suddenly buried his face in the fragrant fall of her hair. 'I've never felt so helpless in my life,' he groaned. 'There was nothing I could do. I made a camp, and kept him as warm as I could—but at dawn the next day, he died.'

Fiercely she held him close to her breast, longing to ease his agonising memories. When next he spoke, his voice was devoid of feeling. 'Two days later I reached Fort Vermilion.'

'And that's your nightmare ... that you were too late to save him.'

'Part of me blames Cheryl, because if he'd never met her, he might still be alive today. But most of all, I blame myself. I should never have let him take off in the first place, knowing how he was feeling. And if I hadn't waited for rescue the first three days after the crash, he might have made it.'

'Heath, you're not God! How could you know what would happen? You did the best you could, under incredibly difficult circumstances.'

'I suppose so,' he said lifelessly.

'Were you hurt in the crash?'

'Yeah, I had a couple of cracked ribs and some cuts and scrapes—haven't you ever noticed the scars?' In the dark he guided her fingers to his ribs, where she could feel the rough cicatrices in his skin.

'So with broken ribs and no doubt a loss of blood, you hauled a full-grown man many miles through some of the wildest bush country in Canada. And you blame yourself! Oh, Heath, you did everything you could.'

'I—I guess you're right. I never really looked at it that way.'

'Well then, it's high time you did. And who knows, Heath—you said Craig wanted to die with his boots on, didn't you? And if he was so deperately in love with Cheryl, would he have got over it?'

'I doubt if he ever would.'

'Maybe he wanted to die ... and he lacked the will to live, neither you nor the best doctors in the world would have saved him.'

Heath raised his head. Rana was relieved to see some of the corroding despair had gone from his face, to be replaced by the quiet dawning of a new hope. 'He did lack the will to live—I see that now,' he said softly.

'And at least the two of you were together at the end. You never abandoned him or left him alone. He must have known how much you loved him.'

'Yeah, I guess he did. Near the end, he thanked me for everything I'd done.'

'So *he* wasn't blaming you.'

'God, no—in fact just the opposite. He felt the crash was his fault.'

'Then get rid of all that guilt you've been carrying for so long, Heath. Believe me, there's no need for you to feel any.'

He stared at her soberly. 'Rana, you're a very wise young woman ... thank you.'

His simple words touched her to the heart, so that she found herself blinking back tears. 'I think you were incredibly brave to do all you did,' she whispered.

'Don't cry.' Propping himself on one elbow, he gazed down at her, pushing back the blanket to expose her body to his view. She was wearing only a filmy lace bra and panties; hungrily his eyes caressed the fullness of her breasts, the slim tapering to her waist, the swell of her hips and thighs. 'You're so beautiful,' he said huskily.

Hypnotised by the naked desire in his face, she lay utterly still, feeling the familiar ache of longing for his touch. Yet it was more than the need for physical pleasure; for the first time in their brief and stormy relationship, she felt that they were coming together as equals. By sharing the tragedy of Craig's death with her, Heath had become real to her in a way no man had ever been before. With all the deep founts of her feminine nature, she longed for fulfilment with him. So when he leaned over to kiss her, her lips met his with his unabashed eagerness, and her hands reached up to tangle in his thick hair, pulling his head closer to hers.

A white fire swept through her, consuming her in its flames. His hands were roving her body, stroking her belly and hips; his hard thighs closed over her limbs. Then his mouth left hers, travelling down her neck to rest on the frantic pulse in her throat. One hand pushed her bra strap from her shoulder, and then his tongue and lips explored the firm roundness of her flesh. Her nipple hardened to his touch. She arched her back with an inarticulate cry of pleasure, pressing herself against him, her nails digging into his skin. He lay across her now, his body crushing her against the blanket. Sensuously she moved her hips under his weight, filled with a primitive glory that she could so arouse him.

'Rana,' she heard him moan. 'Oh God, how I want you!'

'I want you, too.'

Abruptly he pulled away, his breathing ragged. In the faint cold light of dawn, she could see beads of sweat on his forehead. With fingers that were trembling, she brushed them away, afterwards holding his face between her hands in a caress that filled the dark pools of her eyes with tenderness. 'Take me, Heath,' she begged.

'Rana, I can't.'

'Please——'

'No, Rana.' Firmly he removed her hands, kissing their palms, and then laying them by her sides.

'Why not?' she cried.

He answered her question with one of his own. 'Where are you going later today, Rana?'

Puzzled, she said, 'Home, I guess,' although Edmonton and the grey stone mansion seemed incredibly remote.

'Exactly. You're going home. Back to your mother and father and Boyd. Back to your normal life, my dear.'

Numbly she stared at him, while the torment in her body slowly subsided. 'I'll never go back to Boyd,' she said with complete conviction.

'Nevertheless, you'll be back in Edmonton in less than twelve hours. I was in danger of forgetting that—and so were you.' He grinned crookedly. 'Much as I would like to grab you by the hair and drag you bodily back to Clearwater in true caveman style, one has to live with the realities ... which include your parents and your upbringing.' He levered himself upright. 'It's almost morning. Let's see if we can get across the creek.'

It was obvious that the subject was closed: there would be no appeal. Nor did Rana know whether to be glad or sorry. That he could assess the situation so analytically only moments after their lovemaking seemed to give him an unfair advantage. She herself felt desperately vulnerable, totally without defence after his storming of her body. Her heart was pounding, while her flesh still burned from his seeking hands.

He had left the jeep, so she slowly fumbled her way into her still damp clothes, running her fingers through her hair in a vain effort to restore it to some sort of order. Grasping at her pride, the only weapon left to her, she resolved that she must appear as cool and controlled as he. So when he returned, she was sitting in her seat, wiping the condensation from the inside of the window with an old rag.

'I don't think we'll have any trouble now,' he said, starting the engine and driving cautiously down the slope. They inched across the creek-bed, axle-deep in water and rough with stones, and then surged triumphantly up the next hill.

It was a sparkling fresh morning, the sky a pale egg-shell blue, the air loud with birdsong. Illogically Rana was filled with sadness that she would have to leave all this beauty and go home. Home ... it was almost as though this place had become her home, she thought, as they reached the clearing by the crystal-watered lake and saw the house nestled under the sheltering pine trees.

'It's only six-thirty,' Heath said pragmatically as he unlocked the door. 'Why don't we try and sleep for a couple of hours?'

She nodded her agreement, and without further ado he went down the hall to his room, closing the door behind him. A wave of exhaustion nearly submerged her. She entered her own room, pulled off her clothes, and fell into bed, asleep almost before her head hit the pillow.

It was past one o'clock when Rana awoke, to find a beam of golden sunlight falling warm on her cheek. She stretched luxuriously, feeling relaxed and at peace. But when she got up and saw herself in the full-length mirror, she gave an exclamation of horror: a more bedraggled creature she had never seen! She turned on the shower and shampooed her hair, blowing it dry into soft, shining waves. She had brought a pants suit with her, its slim-fitting trousers and jerkin a pale mint green. Worn with a figured silk blouse and artfully applied make-up, it made her look reassuringly elegant and self-possessed.

She made her way to the kitchen, from whence issued mouth-watering odours of bacon and coffee. Heath was busy at the stove. 'Good afternoon!' he said cheerily, only slightly emphasising the second word. 'Help yourself to coffee.'

Cupping the steaming mug in her fingers, she perched on a stool by the window, her eyes wandering with unconscious wistfulness over the vista of sun-drenched lake and forest.

'Did you enjoy the weekend?' Heath asked abruptly.

'Yes, of course!'

There was no doubting her sincerity. His eyes narrowed in calculation, but she was gazing out of the window again and did not see. He opened his mouth to speak, hesitated and said in nearly normal tones, 'How many pancakes can you eat?'

'Dozens!' she laughed, noticing nothing amiss.

They ate crisp bacon and golden pancakes soaked in maple syrup, until finally Rana leaned back, replete. 'I've made an absolute pig of myself! They were delicious, thank you.'

'You're welcome. We'd better clean up. We'll have to leave within the hour if I'm to have you home by dark.'

Her face fell. 'So soon?' she murmured.

'You don't want to go, do you?'

She glanced at him in surprise, for he had spoken with unwonted sharpness. 'I guess I don't,' she admitted honestly. Cupping her chin in her hands, she watched a pair of blue jays squabble over some seeds in the bird feeder on a nearby tree, their plumage iridescent in the sun.

'Rana, will you marry me?'

For a minute she was sure she had imagined his words, so startling were they. Her eyes flew to his face, with its tautly held mouth; his relentless gaze held her pinioned. She said warmly, 'If that's your idea of a joke, Heath Markland, I don't think it's a very funny one.'

'Who said anything about a joke?'

'You're not serious!'

'I was never more serious in my life.'

'But—you're really asking me to marry you?'

'Yes.'

'You're a man of few words!' she exclaimed in exasperation. 'Of course I can't marry you.'

'Why not?'

'Heath, what do you expect me to say?' She began ticking off her fingers one by one. 'I've known you exactly three days—and it's been a relationship with, you have to admit, its ups and downs. We know almost nothing about each other. And we don't love each other.'

'I'll deal with the last objection first. I didn't say I loved you.' He laughed mirthlessly. 'I saw what happened to Craig because of Cheryl—do you expect me to fall in love after that? But I desire you, Rana. I want you in my bed. And it seems the only way I can accomplish that is to marry you.'

'The answer's no!' she cried, fury crackling in every line of her slim figure. 'How cold-blooded can you get!'

'I'm not cold-blooded and you know it,' he said with menacing softness, walking around to her side of the table and lifting her to her feet. Almost brutally he claimed her mouth, while his hands roamed over her body with bruising strength. She fought against him, but in vain. Her lips parted in surrender, while her body curved to fit the contour of his.

He thrust her away. 'Don't deny what happens every time we get near each other, Rana. Marry me, and let me make love to you. You want it as much as I do.'

'No!' she panted, trying to free herself from the cruel grip of his fingers.

'And besides,' he continued inexorably, as though she had never spoken, 'there's Clearwater. You love it too, I can tell. You could live here all the time. When I go away on business trips, I'd take you with me, but we'd always come home to Clearwater.'

'I do like it here, but I can't marry you just because of that.'

'One last thing—by marrying me, you'd be free of your mother. You could visit her, of course, but you wouldn't have to live continually in her shadow, trying to fulfil all her expectations. You'd have your own life that would be nothing to do with her.'

She closed her eyes, pushing him away with all her strength. His arguments, so shrewdly chosen, battered at her defences, until she almost surrendered. She could stay in Clearwater, and be independent of her mother ... and the mere thought of sharing Heath's bed filled her with a wild, sweet joy.

'Do you remember the roses, Rana?'

'Yes, I remember them.'

'It's your choice—retreat into the safe world of your childhood, or take the risk and marry me.'

'But red roses are for love!' she cried tempestuously.

'Grow up, Rana—romance is fine for teenagers, but we're both beyond that. I won't make you pretty speeches, or swear to love you until I die ... but I'll give you excitement and adventure—and passion.'

'And what if there are children?' she blurted. 'Will you love them?'

His face altered, and she saw in it a strange hunger. Speaking more to himself than to her, he said, 'I want a son. What's the point of life if you can't pass on to your own flesh and blood all you've strived for? Give me a son, Rana, and I'll be everlastingly grateful to you.'

I don't want your gratitude, she thought fiercely, feeling her tenuous self-control stretching to breaking point. 'Heath, I can't marry you,' she said with desperate finality. 'I'll go and pack now.'

She whirled and fled to her room, where she pressed ice-cold fingers against her burning cheeks. She had done the right thing, the only thing, by rejecting his proposal. Why then did she feel so shaken and afraid and unhappy? Unable to answer her own questions, she busied herself folding her garments carefully into her case, until she had removed all traces of her brief occupancy from the charming room. Would she ever sleep here again? It did not seem likely. She sighed miserably, and went to put her case in the jeep.

Three hours later Heath turned into the driveway of Rana's home. The house was brilliantly lit, and with a sinking heart she saw cars lined up by the garage; they had visitors. At least Boyd's car wasn't among them.

She and Heath had talked only in monosyllables all the way home. Now she turned to face him uncertainly. 'Thank you, Heath,' she faltered. 'I——'

His eyes twin flecks of flint, he said bluntly, 'I'm staying at the same hotel as last week. I have business appointments most of the day tomorrow, so I'll be there until about four-thirty. The offer's open until then. If you change your mind, you can get in touch with me. If not, don't expect to hear from me again ... I won't grovel for you or any woman, Rana.'

There seemed nothing she could say. She got out of the car, took her case from him, and said goodbye as levelly as she was able, her throat tight with unshed tears. Then she walked steadily towards the door of her home, a slight, lonely figure in the dusk. He drove away, not looking back.

CHAPTER FIVE

AFTER Heath left her, Rana spent the evening in the company of a group of her parents' friends, which at least spared her any inquisitions on the subject of the weekend. All evening as she made light conversation and gave every appearance of a carefree young woman, her thoughts were circling in her mind like caged animals ... Heath wanted her, but only on his terms—in a loveless marriage. It wouldn't work ... it couldn't work. So why didn't she just forget his offer, forget him, and get on with her life? Yet she could not. His image was continually in front of her eyes ... his ruggedly handsome face with its thatch of wheat-gold hair and granite-grey eyes. And the mere memory of their lovemaking had the power to make her nerves quiver and her body ache with desire.

She did not sleep well. In the black hours of the night, his deadline assumed the proportions of a nightmare. She could not marry him, yet equally she could not bear to have him leave her life for ever. She was trapped . . .

Nor did things look better in the morning, as traditionally they were supposed to. Listlessly she trailed down the stairs, feeling tired and heavy-eyed, a cloud of depression hovering over her. She made herself a cup of coffee and went to sit in the living room, where the sun was streaming through the windows. Gratefully she absorbed its heat, finding temporary relief from the cruel dilemma that faced her.

'There you are, Rana! I've been looking for you everywhere,' said Dorothea reproachfully.

'Morning, Mother.'

'It doesn't look as though your weekend was a great success.'

Rana made an effort to conjure up some enthusiasm. 'It was fine. The countryside is beautiful up there, and I enjoyed the plane trips.'

Shrewdly Dorothea did not press her point. 'Well, now that you're back, there's lots to do,' she said briskly. 'I was talking to Boyd on Saturday and he said he'd drop in this evening. He's very anxious to see you, of course.' She took a slip of paper out of her pocket. 'I believe I've worded this correctly. What do you think?'

With a sense of foreboding that was all too soon justified, Rana stared at the neat array of typewritten words. 'Mr and Mrs Richard Liscombe are pleased to announce the engagement of their only daughter Rana Margaret to Boyd Edward Dexter . . .' The letters blurred before her eyes.

Too upset to be tactful, she said sharply, 'Mother, will you please understand once and for all that I am not going to marry Boyd!'

'I've had enough of your nonsense, Rana! You most certainly will marry him.'

Thoroughly angry, Rana crumpled the announcement in her hand. 'You cannot make me do something I don't want to do. I'm not a child any more.'

'I must warn you, Rana, if you persist in being so headstrong and disobedient, how much you are upsetting and worrying your father. He's not at all well, you know. It would put his mind to rest to see you happily settled with Boyd.'

Cold fingers squeezed Rana's heart. 'Not at all well? What do you mean?'

'Dr Harper had as much as said he won't be responsible for the consequences if Richard doesn't slow down at work and relax more at home; he has Richard on a strict diet and a programme of regular exercise. Your father is not a young man any more. The selfish way you've behaved the last few days—ever since you met Heath Markland, as a matter of fact—causes him great concern.'

'Mother,' Rana said in a thin voice scarcely recognisable as her own, 'Daddy would be the last person on earth to want me to marry someone I don't love. Because he loves you, you've had a happy marriage. Surely both of you want the same for me?'

'I've never known you to be so stubborn and wilful,' Dorothea snapped, finally losing her temper. 'You have until tonight to straighten yourself out. Perhaps Boyd can talk some sense into you. I certainly can't!' She stalked out of the room, her heels rapping an angry tattoo on the oak floor.

The second ultimatum for the day, Rana thought with a desperate kind of humour. But she could not lighten her mood for long. Was her father ill, as Dorothea had suggested? Unquestionably he had aged in the last year. Surely if she told him honestly how she felt, he would understand; he would not force her to marry Boyd against her wishes. On impulse she went to the phone and dialled Richard's office, only to be informed by his secretary that he was at meetings all day and had a prior lunch engagement. So that was that.

An oft-repeated remedy of Rana's for her childhood and adolescent woes had been a spell in the garden, weeding or transplanting under the eagle eye of old Tom, the gardener. So now she went outside. In the tool shed she equipped herself with a trowel and a hoe, and headed for the perennial border. It was soothing, repetitive labour with the sun beating on her back and the trills of a robin in her ears; gradually her harassed spirit felt more at peace.

The bitter arguments she had had with Heath, his cynicism, and his businesslike proposal, all dropped away from her; she remembered only the fun they had had canoeing and fishing ... the wild abandon of their lovemaking ... the night they had spent together in the jeep, when he had shared with her his guilt and pain, and had so clearly demonstrated to her his courage and strength.

Kneeling on the edge of the lawn, she stared unseeingly at the tall spikes of the delphiniums, which ranged from palest blue to deep purple. A bee was busily going from flower to flower, its body dusted with pollen. For the rest of her life she would remember those delphiniums and the drowsy humming of the bee.

It was as though scales fell from her eyes; for the first time since meeting Heath, she saw clearly into her heart. She loved him, she thought incredulously. That was why she knew with such absolute clarity that she could never marry Boyd. It was also why she had gone with Heath for the weekend, in spite of all the dictates of caution and good sense that had argued against it. And it was why her body trembled at his touch and leaped into such blazing passion at his nearness ... she loved him.

She put her head on her knees, closing her eyes, while a deep glow of happiness enveloped her. All uncertainty and indecision fell away from her to be replaced by a crystal clarity. Her body and soul were Heath's. She would marry him and live with him in the wild beauty of Clearwater.

The sun passed behind a cloud. A light wind rippled across her shoulders, bare above her brief halter top and shorts. She shivered, wondering what the time was; she had been out quite a while, and Heath had said he would be leaving at four-thirty.

Panic seized her. She scrambled to her feet, dropping the trowel on the ground, and ran for the house. Even as she entered, she could hear the deep chimes of the grandfather clock in the hall . . . four o'clock. Taking the stairs two at a time, she raced to her bedroom, grabbing her car keys and handbag. No time to change. Out in the garage she fitted the key into the ignition with shaking fingers—what if she missed him? There would be no appeal from his ultimatum, she knew him well enough for that. The mere thought of never seeing him again made her break into a cold sweat. She had to get there in time, that was all there was to it.

Driving with an icy precision, she whipped in and out of the traffic. The afternoon rush hour had started and lines of cars were drawn up at every traffic light. Red, yellow, green . . . in an agony of impatience, she tapped her fingernails on the wheel, inching the car forward at a snail's pace. Yellow, red . . . she had missed the light again.

Downtown the tie-ups were worse. Taxis blew their horns, while pedestrians scurried between the stationary vehicles. Rana looked at her watch. Four twenty-five. Her nerves screaming with frustration, she looked around desperately. Then she saw her chance. She swung across the inside lane of traffic, ignoring the loud imprecations of a truck driver, and inched her car into an empty parking space. Not bothering to put money in the meter, she swung her handbag over her shoulder and darted across the road. The hotel was only two blocks away . . . she pushed through the swing door and approached the desk, her heart pounding in her breast now that the moment of truth had come. 'Mr Markland?' she faltered. 'Has he checked out yet?'

Taking what seemed like an inordinately long time, the clerk checked his ledger. 'Markland . . . he should still be here, unless he's left the key in his room. It's Room 1210, ma'am.'

She gasped her thanks and ran for the elevator. With excruciating slowness it carried her to the twelfth floor. She got out and sped down the corridor. The door to 1210 was closed, nor could she hear a sound. Almost suffocating with fear, she raised her hand and knocked sharply with her knuckles. There was no answer.

It took the last vestige of her courage to knock again. With a suddenness that made her jump the door swung open. Heath stood there, a towel knotted around his waist, his wet hair plastered to his skull, and rivulets of water running down his chest and legs. His face expressionless, he waited for her to speak.

'I—I thought you'd gone,' Rana whispered, then burst into tears.

She felt him guide her into the room and heard the door shut. He sat her on the bed and produced a large white handkerchief. 'What's wrong?' he asked; she had by now recovered sufficiently to discern the almost clinical detachment of his voice.

She opened her mouth to say, 'I love you. I want to marry you.' But something stopped her, and dumbstruck she gazed up at him, her breath still catching in her throat in ragged sighs. Slowly her brain began to function again. Heath had never said he loved her, she now realised, in fact he had taken pains to indicate he never would. He wanted a woman for his bed and a mother for his children, that was all. It was a sickening blow to her pride to recognise that she would marry him on any terms . . . she could not bear to live without him.

Swallowing hard, she said, 'My mother won't leave me alone, Heath, she keeps on and on at me to marry Boyd. He's supposed to ask me again this evening. And she says my father's ill, and it's partly my fault, and I mustn't worry him . . .' Her voice trailed away uncertainly, for Heath was regarding her with a narrow-eyed watchfulness that unnerved her.

'What am I supposed to do?'

This was far worse than she could possibly have anticipated. She tried to stand up, but her knees seemed to have turned to water, so that she collapsed back on the bed. 'You said you'd marry me,' she stammered. 'If you still want me—then I'll marry you.'

'I see.' He rubbed the stubble on his chin absently, the muscles in his chest rippling under the sun-bronzed skin.

Her heart began to pound again, in sick, heavy strokes. It was no good, she thought numbly. He had changed his mind. An appalling vista of loneliness opened up in front of her.

'Why are you dressed like that?'

His question came as a total surprise. She glanced down at herself, seeing her bare feet in flat, thonged sandals, her brief denim shorts and coloured halter top. Her hands and fingernails were caked with mud.

'You have dirt on your face too,' he commented, impersonally scrubbing at her cheek with the handkerchief.

'I was weeding in the garden. That was when I decided to come and see you,' she answered, more or less truthfully. 'But it was the rush hour and I was afraid you'd be gone.'

Still with that odd watchfulness on his face, he drew her upright. 'Put your arms around me,' he ordered. 'Now kiss me.'

Trembling from nervous strain, she stood on tiptoes and brushed his lips with hers.

Harshly he said, 'You can do better than that, Rana.'

A tiny flame of anger burst into life within her. If he was going to turn her down, he would at least know what he'd be missing, she thought furiously. With deliberate sensuality she moved her palms up his rib cage, and across the broad expanse of his torso, running her fingers through the damply curling mat of hair on his chest. She pressed herself against him in provocative invitation, then began to kiss him.

With ruthless speed he seized the initiative from her. He threw her back across the bed, his hard body crushing her into the covers, his mouth brutally ravaging hers. As he thrust one hand under her halter top, she cried out in shameless pleasure, digging her nails into his flesh to draw him closer, vibrantly aware of the pressure of his thighs between her legs. Her world dissolved into a maelstrom of unfulfilled longing.

With a shock like a shower of cold water, she felt Heath wrench himself free of her embrace. 'You're sure you want to go through with this marriage, Rana?'

Her breath shivered in her throat from his merciless assault. 'Y-yes,' she whispered . . . she had no choice.

'You want to be rid of Boyd and your mother. I want to make love to you—and I want a son.' She stared at him wordlessly, like a wild creature threatened by a hunter. 'Am I right?' he demanded.

'Yes.'

'Good. As long as we understand each other.'

She smothered an almost hysterical giggle, so little did he understand her motives.

He paused and went on thoughtfully, 'What's today—Monday? I fly to Vancouver tomorrow and I'll get back Thursday afternoon. So I guess it'll have to be Thursday evening. I can make the arrangements before I leave.'

She had recovered sufficiently to say with more than a hint of sarcasm, 'You might ask if I'm free that evening. I do happen to be involved in this too.'

'I assumed you'd want to get married as soon as possible,' was the cool response.

She could not refute his maddening logic. 'I do.' She stared down at her clenched fingers. 'But however will I tell my mother?'

'I suggest you don't. After we're married, we can tell her together.'

'She'll be furious,' Rana said in a small voice.

'I have no doubt. But it will be too late by then, won't it?'

This had an ominous ring. 'She's expecting me to get engaged to Boyd this evening.'

'Can't you stave them off?' he said impatiently. 'Tell them you want a week to think about it, and that they're to leave you alone while you do so.'

'I could do that. It doesn't seem very honest.'

'With people like your mother, I'm not sure you can afford the luxury of honesty.' He moved away from the bed. 'That's settled then, is it? I'll give you a call Thursday afternoon as soon as I land. We can meet somewhere downtown.'

Rana was increasingly tempted to change her mind, so repelling was his manner; she had never known him to be so cold and distant. Like every girl, she had done her share of day-dreaming, and had always imagined herself floating up the aisle in a cloud of white tulle to a man who adored her. The reality would obviously be very different. 'I want to be married in a church,' she said stubbornly.

'So you will be. A good friend of mine is a clergyman. And don't look so worried,' he added. 'A considerable number of marriages start out on a lot worse foundation than ours will—we're two adults who know what we want and who aren't deceiving ourselves with a lot of moonshine.'

'A considerable number of marriages end up in the divorce court, too,' she said astringently.

'Well, ours won't! Let's get that straight right now. I'm old-fashioned, Rana. Marriage is for life as far as I'm concerned. If you disagree, you'd better say so now.'

Divorce him, when she loved him with all her heart? The thought was inconceivable. 'I quite agree with you,' she said coolly. Then her treacherous tongue continued with more than a touch of wistfulness, 'But I always did want to get married in white.'

For a moment the Heath of Clearwater, the friendly,

teasing companion, reappeared. 'You could surely sneak down the back stairs in a short white dress without anyone getting suspicious, couldn't you?'

'I guess so,' she chuckled, immeasurably relieved. But her consolation was short-lived.

'And now you'd better go,' he said. 'I have to go out shortly, and as you can see, I'm not ready.'

It was plain he had no intention of saying where he was going, or with whom. Would he be with another woman? A hot stab of jealousy, an emotion hitherto unknown to her, ripped through her. Fighting for self-control, she stood up. 'Goodbye,' she said, inwardly crying out for reassurance that she was doing the right thing with this precipitous marriage.

But he gave her none. His flint-grey eyes still strangely watchful, he said, 'Goodbye, Rana.'

She picked up her handbag and left the room, her slim figure invested with a lonely dignity. She would neither beg for comfort, nor allow herself the luxury of tears; not in front of the hard-eyed stranger who in three short days would become her husband . . .

CHAPTER SIX

SOMEHOW the three days passed. Feeling as though she were in limbo, Rana told both Boyd and her mother that she needed a week to think about her future plans; she spoke with calm detachment and a sense of authority that neither could penetrate. Baffled by her daughter's newly found maturity, Dorothea could only accept Rana's terms, including the firmly worded injunction that Rana be left alone to make her decision.

Rana did manage to get five minutes alone with Richard, although this was not easy; it was almost as though Dorothea guessed her intention, and deliberately set out to foil any meeting between father and daughter. But late Wednesday evening, Rana found her father in the library at a time when she knew Dorothea was on the phone. 'Daddy,' she said urgently, going right to the heart of the matter, 'I truly don't wish to worry you or cause you concern. But you wouldn't want me to marry someone I don't love, would you?'

'You mean Boyd?' he said heavily.

With compunction she saw the new lines on his face, the almost defeated slope of his shoulders. 'Yes, I do. I'm fond of him—but he's more like a brother to me than a prospective husband.'

'Your mother has her heart set on this marriage.'

'I know that only too well.'

'Don't you think she might know what's best for you, Rana?'

It was on the tip of her tongue to say, 'No! I'm tired of her domination. I want to live my own life!' But she bit back the hasty words, knowing they would only hurt her father, blind as he was to Dorothea's faults.

'She has your best interests at heart, you know,' Richard went on gently. 'Boyd's a fine man, and a good lawyer. He can give you security and the kind of life to which you are accustomed. You're young, Rana, perhaps too young to realise how important these rather mundane things can be.'

'Yes, Daddy,' she said unhappily, seeking to end the conversation; she loved her father dearly for his gentleness and concern, but was almost sure he would never emerge from behind Dorothea's shadow, nor go against her wishes, not even for his only daughter's sake. She patted him on the sleeve, wanting only to protect him from further strife. However, she knew that was impossible, for tomorrow she would secretly become the wife of Heath Markland, a man whom Dorothea feared and despised. She dropped a kiss on his cheek. 'I'm going to bed, I'm tired.' Scared by his appearance of fragility, she added, 'Take care of yourself, Daddy. And remember that I love you.'

Totally misunderstanding her frame of mind, he said with relief, 'I'm glad you're seeing reason, my dear. I'm sure Boyd will make you very happy. Goodnight.'

Feeling very much alone, Rana went to her room, to sit staring out into the shadowed quiet of the garden. It was the last night she would spend alone, for tomorrow night she would be Heath's . . . a shiver of fear ran along her over-stretched nerves. She was afraid, afraid of her own vulnerability and of the power he had over her. Would she ever be able to tell him she loved him? Would he, in time, come to understand she was not another Cheryl, to abandon the man she had loved when he needed her? In the empty darkness of the night, neither prospect seemed very likely, and before she slept, her pillow was damp with tears.

However, the next day events played into her hands; her parents had been invited out for dinner, but would be returning fairly early in the evening. And luckily she herself was by the telephone when Heath called. Its shrill ring made her jump. Instinctively she knew it would be Heath. 'Hello?' she said in a voice thin with tension.

'Rana? Heath here. Can you meet me at St Michael's Church at eight? Do you know where it is?'

'Yes,' she said, her throat dry; for the past three days she had been intermittently haunted by the nightmare that he might have changed his mind.

'Are you still there? You sound very far away.'

'Yes, I'm still here,' she said idiotically, her palm on the receiver slippery with perspiration.

'Will your parents be home?'

'They're going out earlier, but they should be back by ten or ten-thirty.'

'Fine! I'll take you out for dinner after the ceremony, and that should time it about right.'

The thought of eating nauseated her, although she

managed to say weakly, 'Thank you.'

'I'll see you at eight then, Rana. Goodbye.' The connection was cut with a decisive click.

Her parents left the house a little after six, at least giving Rana the chance to be by herself for a while; it had been a strain trying to behave as though today was a day like any other. As she looked at herself in the mirror, her stomach was fluttering with apprehension, her eyes huge in a pinched, pale face.

But she was not Eli's granddaughter for nothing. Defiance stirred within her. Maybe she was making a terrible mistake to marry Heath Markland and maybe she would regret her hasty decision in the months and years to come ... but even if this was true, she would not go to her wedding looking like a ghost at a funeral. So she soaked in a luxuriously hot bath, and then made up her face with painstaking care—a touch of rouge on her cheeks, eye-shadow of palest blue emphasising the beauty of her long-lashed azure eyes. She applied soft coral lipstick and surveyed herself dispassionately—that was better.

She had bought a new dress in one of the downtown boutiques, and now she carefully removed it from its protective polythene bag. It was designed of ivory shantung in a shirtwaist style, with a full skirt, and wide sleeves gathered tightly at the wrist with tiny buttons. Its high collar and deep V-neckline, by their very severity, subtly called attention to her firm young breasts and the fragile beauty of her face. She slipped her feet into daintily strapped sandals of the same shade of ivory, and picked up her evening bag. She was ready ...

Afterwards Rana was to remember only brief snatches of the next two hours ... the swift flare of passion in Heath's eyes as he watched her walk up the church steps towards him ... the gentleness of his fingers, so at variance with the sternness of his face, as he pinned an exquisite corsage of dark red roses to her dress ... the triumphant peal of the organ after the all too brief ceremony that made them man and wife ... the subdued elegance of the restaurant to which he took her for dinner ... her dizziness from drinking too much champagne while only nibbling at her food ... the silent drive through the city streets to her parents' home ... the dazed expression on Dorothea's face as she saw Heath and Rana enter the door together, Rana in a white dress with flowers pinned to her shoulder ...

'I didn't know you were going out with Mr Markland tonight, Rana.'

Forestalling Rana's reply, Heath said smoothly, 'I purposely suggested Rana not to tell you, Mrs Liscombe. We've come to ask your blessing; your daughter did me the honour of becoming my wife this evening.'

Her face ashen, Dorthea repeated, 'Your wife?'

'Yes, we were married two hours ago.'

'Rana, it isn't true?'

'Yes, Mother.'

'But why on earth did you do it?'

'Heath can give me so much that Boyd can't—please do try and understand.'

'You foolish girl! You've thrown away every chance for a decent marriage. How could you behave so deceitfully?'

'I must take the blame for the secrecy, Mrs Liscombe,' Heath interposed, steel-voiced and obviously not intimidated by Dorothea's rage. 'We were afraid you would react in just this way—so I insisted Rana keep silent beforehand.'

'I'll have it annulled!'

'As Rana is over eighteen, that's impossible.'

The door opened and Richard walked in, looking in bewilderment from his wife's furious demeanour to Rana's pleading face. 'Richard!' Dorothea exploded. 'Your daughter has married Heath Markland!'

For a brief instant Richard's eyes sought Heath's, a desperate question in their depths. Heath nodded, as though in reassurance, and perceptibly Richard's rigid hold on himself relaxed. It was an odd little incident, one which Rana was to recall only several days later.

'Now, Dorothea,' Richard said, an unusual firmness in his voice, 'you know as well as I do that the child was dead set against marrying Boyd. You may not care for the idea of this marriage right now, but I'm sure in time you'll come to accept it, and to accept Heath as your son-in-law. He can, I'm sure, offer Rana every material advantage.'

Her father's unexpected support filled Rana with gratitude. She ran across the room and hugged him with all her strength. 'Thank you, Daddy!'

For once Dorothea was speechless. Imperturbably Richard rang for Henson. 'This calls for champagne,' he said. So for the second time in as many hours, Rana gulped down the heady liquid, while the four of them maintained a somewhat stilted conversation.

Finally Heath stood up. 'We'll be going to Clearwater tomorrow, but I have to fly to Calgary on Sunday on business. Perhaps we can have dinner together on the way back.' Again a look of silent complicity was exchanged between the two men; they walked out into the hall, leaving Rana and Dorothea together.

'No matter what your father says,' Dorothea hissed, 'I will never accept this marriage—you've ruined your life!'

'You're exaggerating——'

'The man's a scoundrel. If I'd known you were contemplating this dreadful step, I would have told you everything I know about him and his family. You'll soon come to realise that money isn't everything.'

Terrified by the undisguised enmity in Dorothea's face, Rana said in a low voice, 'I wish you hadn't taken it this way . . . truly he's a good man, Mother.'

'He's a ruthless opportunist. You're the victim——'

'Coming, Rana?'

Shaken to the core, Rana gave her mother's unresponsive cheek a quick kiss, and hugged her father.

'I'll see you both next week,' she whispered. Then, mercifully, they were outside, and she was beyond the reach of Dorothea's venomous tongue.

All too soon for Rana, they reached Heath's hotel; the events of the past few hours had by now caught up with her, and she was taut with nervous tension. As they rode up in the elevator, she stole a glance at the formidable man by her side. What did she really know of him? What did her mother know, of which she, Rana, was ignorant?

The only sure knowledge was that she, who loved, was not loved in return. This had not seemed to matter too much three days ago, but now it assumed the proportions of a nightmare. She wished she did not feel so frightened ... somehow she had assumed they would go to Clearwater immediately, and intuitively she knew that in Clearwater things would be different, for Clearwater felt like home.

The impersonal bareness of the hotel room struck her as they entered. A few of Heath's toilet articles lay scattered on the dresser, and his raincoat had been left on the bed; that was all. There was a brocade-covered chesterfield beneath the wide expanse of window which looked over the lights of the city; she leaned against it and looked out, swallowing nervously. Soundlessly Heath came up behind her, putting his arms around her waist. She jumped in fright and instinctively pulled away from him. 'I—I think I'll have a shower.'

'Don't be too long.'

She took what she needed out of her suitcase and went into the bathroom, locking the door behind her, and savouring the relief of being alone. Taking as long as she could, she showered and put on a matching nightdress and housecoat of pale blue chiffon. Finally she knew she could delay no longer. When she came back in the room, Heath was propped up in bed watching television; he had already discarded his shirt and tie. She felt a stab of resentment that he should look so relaxed and at ease.

Absently he patted the bed. 'Sit a minute,' he suggested. 'I just want to hear the results of the by-election.'

She perched awkwardly on the bed, her fingers restlessly plucking at the filmy fabric of her housecoat. She was lonelier than she had ever been in her life, and would have given almost anything to have found herself back home in the familiar surroundings of her own room ... alone; she did not want to make love with a man who did not love her.

The announcer's voice droned on, and finally Heath gave an exclamation of satisfaction. 'Great! I hoped he'd get in—he's a good man.' He got up and switched off the television. Walking around to Rana's side of the bed, he stood staring down at her. 'Hello, my beautiful Rana.'

She stared at her clenched hands, her hair falling like a curtain around her pale face.

'From the first moment I saw you, I wanted to possess you,' he said exultantly. 'You were standing in Eli's office with the sun a halo around your head ... you looked so cool and correct in your grey dress. I wanted to bring you to life, awaken you to passion. It was only a week ago—but it seems as though I've waited a lifetime for this moment. Stand up, Rana, and look at me.'

She got to her feet. She felt icy-cold and somehow detached from her body. A wave of dizziness attacked her, and she blinked it back. From a long way away she felt his hands come round her body. Then his mouth found hers. She was drowning in his kiss, unable to breathe, as another wave of faintness almost submerged her. With all her strength she pushed him away. 'Don't!' she gasped. 'Please don't.'

His fingers bit into her shoulders through the thin fabric of her gown. 'What do you mean—don't?'

Too frightened to be tactful, she cried, 'I don't want you to touch me!'

'Rana, you're my wife now.'

'I know. But——'

'We're married,' he reiterated. 'Remember?'

'You're not going to let me forget, are you?' In vain she tried to free herself from his vice-like grip.

'I hadn't imagined you'd want to forget,' he said bitingly. 'Not this soon, anyway.' He bent his head as though to kiss her again, but there was no mistaking her frantic move to evade him. His eyes narrowed, and she shivered at their bleak menace. 'Rana, for the last time, kiss me.'

'No! I don't want to!'

'For God's sake!' he exploded, releasing her so suddenly that she swayed on her feet. 'What do I have to do to break through that shell of yours?'

Panic closed her throat. She had escaped one cage only to be trapped in another, for she had married this cold-eyed stranger and thereby given him a husband's rights to her body. How could she blame him if he wanted to claim those rights? She made a desperate effort to break through the web of fear that bound her. 'It's just that I'm——'

But he did not hear her, for the thin thread of his patience had snapped. Cat-swift, he caught her in a brutally strong embrace. One hand entangled in her hair, he forced her head backwards and began kissing her mercilessly.

All Rana's fears of the unknown world into which she was venturing rose up and overwhelmed her. Her heart fluttered against her ribs like a trapped bird. An icy sweat broke out on her forehead. Darkness swept over and engulfed her, and her body crumpled bonelessly in his arms . . .

She was struggling up out of a smothering blackness, fleeing from an unknown terror . . . when she opened her eyes, she looked straight into Heath's and caught in them a swiftly masked expression of naked pain. Bewildered, she tried to sit up, but with deliberate firmness he pushed her back on the pillows. 'You fainted,' he said matter-of-factly.

'I'm sorry,' she faltered, 'I don't know why I did that. I never faint.'

'Don't try and talk now,' he continued, so impersonally that she was chilled rather than reassured. 'Just go to sleep.'

'But, Heath——'

'I won't bother you any more. I'll sleep on the chesterfield.'

Too tired and weak to argue, she curled up on her side, dimly aware that he was pulling the blankets over her shoulders. Drained of all emotion, she fell asleep almost immediately.

When she awoke, it was broad daylight; so deep and dreamless had been her slumber that she had scarcely disturbed the bedding. Then the events of the night before rushed into her consciousness, and shamefaced, she buried her head in the pillow.

'Are you awake, Rana?'

Taking her courage in her hands, she turned over to face Heath—Heath, her husband, although only in name. He was fully dressed. She said in a small voice, 'Good morning. You're up early.'

'It's nearly nine,' he replied coolly. 'Why don't you get up and get dressed?'

'What are we going to do?'

'We'll go to Clearwater.'

'Heath, I——'

'Don't talk now, Rana. Let's just get there as quickly as we can.'

She sensed that he was holding tightly to his self-control. 'All right,' she acquiesced.

Within an hour they had reached the airport, and a scant two hours later the jeep rounded the last corner in the road and Clearwater came into sight. Neither of them had said much on the journey, restricting themselves to remarks about the weather and the state of the road. But now as Rana climbed out of the jeep and stretched her cramped legs, she said spontaneously, 'I'm so glad we've come, Heath! It was a good idea of yours.'

He took a minute to survey the circle of enclosing hills and the still waters of the lake, sparkling in the midday sun. 'Put on your jeans and throw a few old clothes in a haversack. I'll look after the supplies.'

'Why? Where are we going?'

'I'm taking you up to my grandfather's cabin—where Craig and I grew up.'

Her spirits, oppressed by the fears and misunderstandings of the night before, began to rise. When she brought her loaded knapsack down to the jetty, Heath had already packed canvas bags of equipment neatly under the gunwales. He stowed her gear with the rest. 'I think that's everything,' he said, more to himself than to her. 'Hope you're feeling energetic. It's a ten-mile trip with a portage half way.'

'You may have to carry me, as well as the canoe!'

He grunted a noncommittal reply; they seated themselves in the canoe and he pushed off from shore. For the next three hours Rana worked harder than she ever had in her life. They paddled steadily up the lake in the face of a light head wind; wavelets slapped at the prow of the canoe, the breeze carrying the mingled scents of water and forest. Heath allowed a brief halt for a meal, producing two box lunches he had obtained at the hotel; then they set off again. By now Rana's muscles were protesting against the unaccustomed exercise, although she persevered, determined not to cry for quarter.

The lake gradually narrowed to a meandering stream, its banks overgrown with tall rushes. A pair of ducks exploded into the air from among the reeds, while on the distant muskeg a moose raised its antlered head, lazily watching their approach before loping off into the low-growing scrub spruce.

The stream became more and more shallow; on Heath's instructions Rana rested her paddle on her knees, keeping a sharp eye for rocks that could damage the canoe. Finally Heath beached the craft, saying, 'We'll portage here. It's about a mile to the next lake.'

They had to make two trips back and forth to carry all the gear as well as the canoe; it was hot and humid, and the mosquitoes and black flies rose in droves from the swampy ground. Although Rana had doused herself in fly dope—a vile-smelling concoction Heath had given her—the insects whined about her head with maddening persistence. It was a relief to get back in the canoe and out on to the water again, although by now her arms and shoulders were aching with tiredness.

After what seemed like hours, Heath said quietly, 'See the strip of sand on the shore up ahead? The cabin's among the trees there.'

Within ten minutes they had arrived. Heath drove the canoe up on the beach and slowly Rana climbed out, wincing with pain as she straightened her back. 'Are you sore?' he asked.

'Sore's not the word,' she said ruefully.

For the first time that day he smiled at her with complete naturalness. The breeze played with his hair, the sun beating on his bronzed face and throat. 'You did well. It was a hard day's work and you didn't complain once.'

She flushed with pleasure, as happiness welled within her. She was putty in this man's hands, she thought with her usual honesty, as she picked up two haversacks and followed Heath up the beach. One smile, and her foolish heart danced in her breast . . . if only last night had never happened.

She was jerked from her reverie by their arrival at the log cabin. Heath unlocked the door and quickly began opening all the windows to air the place. The interior was dry and clean, simply furnished with double bunks, a wood stove, and homemade table and chairs. Rana looked around quietly, her vivid imagination peopling the room with the bearded Sam Markland and his two small grandsons; because Heath had grown up here; she felt immediately at home.

She helped him unpack, taking a childish delight in stacking their food on the shelves and shaking out the bedding. Then while Heath chopped kindling outside, the bite of his axe ringing through the woods, she wandered along the shore picking a bunch of wildflowers, which she then arranged in a jar on the kitchen table.

'The woman's touch,' Heath teased her gently, as he carried in an armload of freshly split wood. 'Do you want to go for a dip in the lake, Rana, while I start supper. You must be tired, and it'll at least wash off the worst of the fly dope.'

Cherishing his concern, she smiled shyly. 'That sounds like a wonderful idea.'

So for almost fifteen minutes she stroked lazily in the lake, the cool water infinitely refreshing. Wrapping a towel over her bikini, she padded back to the cabin. Heath, stripped to the waist now, was still outside at the woodpile. She addressed him gratefully, 'I feel like a new woman.' Unpinning her hair from the crown of her head so that it fell to her shoulders, she tried not to let her eyes linger on the tanned expanse of his chest with its smooth play of muscles.

'You look beautiful.'

Their eyes met, and she saw in his the burning intensity of his desire for her. Yet he made no move towards her, holding himself under rigid control. With all the deep generosity of her nature, she knew this was wrong. 'Heath,' she said quietly, 'I'm so sorry about last night. To start with, I let my mother upset me. And I was frightened too, because I've never made love before. I didn't mean to hurt you.'

His gaze softened, wandering over her face in a tender caress. 'I'm sorry too—it was just as much my fault. I was far too rough with you.'

Deliberately she let the towel slide to the ground and

stood still, the sunlight dappling her skin, her eyes dark, mysterious pools. Slowly he walked towards her, his footsteps muffled by the turf. From the thick underbrush came the lilting melody of a thrush.

Almost as though he was afraid to touch her, he tentatively kissed her upturned face. Sensing his hesitation, she slid her fingers up his bare chest and around his neck, pulling his head down. His second kiss drained the strength from her body; when it was over they were both breathing hard. As his hands, warm and sure, slid down the curve of her spine and gathered her body closer to his masculine hardness, her love for this man rose up within her so that her eyes were flooded with an unconscious yearning. His lips rained kisses on her cheeks, throat, and on the wet skin of her shoulders. 'You taste of lake water,' he murmured. 'I want you so much, girl.'

'And I want you, Heath,' she said as steadily as she could, while tremors of desire quivered through her limbs.

He gazed deeply into her eyes, as though searching for her very soul. 'Let me make you mine,' he whispered huskily. Bravely she held his gaze, although warm colour reddened her cheeks; he could read on her face her longing for surrender.

With a muffled exclamation he swung her into his arms, and carried her over the threshold of the little cabin, kicking the door shut behind him ... from deep in the woods came the rippling echo of the thrushes' song.

Afterwards, spent by the tumult of their lovemaking, Rana must have slept. When she opened her eyes, it was to see Heath leaning on one elbow, his big body arching protectively over hers. Remembering the storm of their mutual passion, she blushed fiercely, her eyelashes fluttering down to hide the telltale sheen of rapture in her eyes.

'Hello, wife,' he said softly.

Her lips curved delightfully. 'So I am,' she said with a note in her voice of such self-satisfaction that he chuckled.

'No regrets?' he asked.

'None.' Their lovemaking had fulfilled all and more of her expectations, for Heath had been a lover of such tenderness and generosity that he had swept away all her fears, instead engulfing her in wonderment and delight.

'There's something I've never told any woman, Rana,' he said slowly. 'I've never told you—and while we were making love, I knew it to be time.'

'What is it?' she whispered.

He clasped her fingers in his and raised them to his lips. His eyes were trained on her face, a light in them such as she had never seen before. 'I love you,' he said with deep seriousness. 'Body and soul, I love you.'

Her lips parted incredulously, and joy blazed in the brilliant azure of her eyes. 'Oh, Heath,' she breathed, 'I love you, too.'

He kissed her with a new, lingering adoration. 'I didn't dare hope you'd love me in return.'

'Nor did I!' she exclaimed with somewhat muddled grammar. 'You seemed so cold and businesslike when you proposed.'

'I was afraid you'd say "no". Which, may I remind you, you did.'

'So I did! But how was I to know you loved me?'

'I fell in love with you the first moment I saw you in your grey dress with your hair like white fire about your face.'

'For a man in love, you were abominably rude!'

'How did you expect me to behave? I swore after Craig died that I'd never fall in love with anyone—and then you walked into my life, Rana Markland, and turned it upside down.'

'As you did with mine,' she said softly. 'How could I marry Boyd after meeting you?' She gave a quick blissful sigh. 'Heath, I'm so happy, it scares me.'

'Don't be scared, sweetheart. We know we love each other, and that we'll always be together—what is there to be scared of?'

Shyly she reached up and traced the chiselled line of his mouth with her fingertip. He nibbled it between his teeth. 'Keep that up, and you never know what might happen,' he threatened, a thread of laughter in his deep voice. Suddenly he pulled her to him, so that her satin-smooth body lay against his bronzed skin. 'Rana, I love you.' Her passion leaped to meet him, and together they journeyed through new worlds of pleasures and delight...

CHAPTER SEVEN

For Rana, the journey back to Clearwater was one of profound contentment. For the first time in her life she felt that she was indeed going home. Home! She belonged with Heath—to Heath—and they would share and build their lives together at Clearwater.

The canoe sliced through the mirror-like surface of the lake, the silence that engulfed them punctuated only by the cry of some distant bird on the far shore, and the dip of their paddles moving in perfect unison. Joy surged within her as she thrilled to the feeling of moving in rhythm with this powerful man who was now her husband. Her arms ached but were not tired. She felt that she could move with him, like this, for ever. Quietly, he watched her reactions to her surroundings and just as quietly said, 'And up on the hill against the sky,

a fir tree rocking its lullaby,
swings, swings
Its emerald wings
swelling the song that my paddle sings.'

She turned to look at him, surprise evident on her

face. 'Why, that's beautiful, Heath. What is it? Where did you ever hear that?'

He laughed gently. 'A poem, one that my grandfather liked quite a bit. What's the matter? Do I surprise you that much, my being able to quote poetry?' he drawled.

'No ... well, yes, in a way. It just doesn't seem that you would pay much attention to things like poetry.'

'Uncultured Heath Markland—a man who only has time for trees and oil—that's the image you have of me, eh, girl?'

She flushed, now uncomfortable and wanting nothing, not even the smallest barrier, to rise between them. 'I didn't mean anything by it. I was surprised, that's all.'

He stopped paddling and smiled back at her. 'Relax. I imagine we'll surprise each other more than a few times, Rana Markland, as we come to know one another.'

Shortly they entered the inlet which protected the house. It stood, hugged by towering pines and surrounded by rolling lawn which ran down to the water's edge, golden and inviting in the early morning sun. I do belong, Rana thought excitedly. I *am* home.

They beached the canoe and unloaded their gear, moving slowly across the lawn in the morning warmth. 'Tired?' asked Heath.

'No, just feeling lazy; lazy and so quiet and peaceful inside.' She sighed shyly. 'I was thinking—on the way back, out there on the lake—how right everything feels ...' She looked up at Heath, trying to gauge his response, unsure of herself, unused to sharing her feelings so openly. 'I ... I never before had the feeling that I had this morning.'

Heath took her gear and piled it on the verandah, his eyes watchful but gentle and flecked with a quiet, waiting light. 'What kind of feeling, Rana?'

'The feeling that ... that I really was coming home. Oh, I don't know, I felt for the first time that I belonged somewhere, that I was a part of something ... of someone.' She could feel the warmth of her cheeks that surely must be flushed, and embarrassed, she turned her eyes from his steadfast gaze.

'Look at me, Rana,' he said quietly, as he reached out and tilted her face to his. 'You have come home,' he breathed fiercely, 'and you do belong—to Clearwater and me.' He drew her into his arms, his desire for her surging within him. 'Rana, Rana ...' he whispered, feeling her instant response.

Moments later he pushed her gently from him. 'Come on, girl, let's get this gear inside, before we end up spending the morning in bed.'

The sound of a jeep interrupted Heath's teasing laughter and they turned to see Bill Stewart, a worker from the lumber camp, pull up beside the house. He slammed the door and moved lethargically towards them, his cold glare insolently appraising Rana, who stood, clad only in shorts and a T-shirt, beside Heath. She felt, rather than saw, Heath stiffen at the man's approach, and moved to withdraw into the house and leave the two men to their business.

Seeing her intention made obvious by her self-conscious movement, Bill drawled rudely, 'Oh, don't run off on my account, Mrs Markland. In fact, I've given up my quiet Sunday morning to do you a favour. I've come to give a message to you, not your husband.'

Heath's flint-hard voice cut through the air and left the other man with no misconceptions about his reception. 'What do you want, Stewart?'

The man straightened and coldly flung his next words at them, 'A Mrs Liscombe from Edmonton has been trying to get hold of Mrs Markland since Friday night. She left word at the camp last night that it's urgent and you'd better get in touch with her right away.'

'Thanks, Stewart, we'll tend to it right away.' Heath turned abruptly, leaving him a clear message of cold dismissal.

It was nearly an hour before Rana was able to get through to Edmonton, her mother's line being busy with each attempt. Finally Dorothea answered, her voice distraught and shrill. 'Where in heaven's name have you been? I've been trying to reach you for two days now.'

'We've ... Heath and I ... we've been out on the river. We left on Friday morning and just got back. We're flying to Calgary this afternoon. Heath has business there. We just got your message. What's wrong, Mother?'

The conversation was brief, more of a monologue from that point on. Then it was over. Slowly replacing the receiver in its cradle, Rana turned, her face ashen grey and stricken with fear, to look at Heath, who stood waiting in the doorway. 'What is it? What's the matter?' he questioned urgently. She leaned weakly against the desk, feeling all of a sudden that she had neither the will nor the strength to answer. In a single swift movement he was at her side steadying her. 'Tell me what's happened, girl?'

'It's Daddy. He's ... he's in hospital. He's had a heart attack—Friday afternoon and ... Mother says ... she says that ... that he's dying and I should come right away. Oh, Heath ...' She dissolved in a flood of tears against his chest. He held her, long moments, not trying to interrupt her weeping but letting it run its course.

Finally, when she was quiet and still against him, he said, 'Okay, what we need to do now is get a few things packed and fly to Edmonton. We'll be there by early afternoon.'

'But you ... you were going away today ... you had business to ... Maybe I should go alone.'

'Hush,' he interrupted her feeble protests. 'It can wait. I'm coming with you.' He wiped her tear-stained face and added gently, 'And don't go back expecting the worst, Rana. Your mother has a tendency to dramatise. Wait and see what the doctors have to say.'

The flight to Edmonton, although only of short duration, seemed an aeon long to Rana. She sat, stiff and restrained, next to Heath, trying to follow his words of caution. Her father would be all right, he had to be all right, she told herself over and over again.

It was nearly one o'clock when they landed in Edmonton and walked quickly through the terminal. 'What hospital is he in, Rana?' Heath's steady voice interrupted her desperate thoughts.

'The Royal Alex, I think ... I'm not sure. Mother said ... Damn ... I don't know, I just can't remember,' she stammered.

'Take it easy. Do you want me to call and check the Alex or would you rather go home first?'

'I don't know ... maybe home.' She turned to him suddenly, her trembling hand grasping at his arm. 'He will be all right, won't he, Heath? Daddy's going to be fine, isn't he?' Her voice was pleading and all she wanted to hear now were his assurances.

Heath drew a deep breath. 'I can't tell you what you want to hear, Rana, as much as I want to. You have to wait and hear what the doctor has to say.' He put an arm around her shoulders and hugged her to him. In spite of his attempt at comforting her, for an instant she was angry at the pragmatism of the man, the pragmatism that would not permit him, even for an instant, to utter the reassuring words she so desperately wanted to hear. But her anger fled as he took her hand in his. 'Come on, I'll take you home and we'll go from there.' He was with her, what else could she possibly need?

He hailed a taxi and in less than a half hour Heath was paying the driver and carrying their bags to the front door. He leaned patiently against one of the tall pillars, as Rana rang the bell. 'Don't tell me it's locked. It's a little like locking Government House, isn't it?' he quipped.

She shrugged. 'Mother always preferred to keep it locked,' then she smiled mischievously at him, 'And yes, it does seem a bit like an institution, doesn't it?'

Presently, the wide door was swung open by Henson, who nodded gravely and stepped back to admit them.

'Good afternoon, Mrs Markland ... and Mr Markland.'
'Hello, Henson. Is my mother at home?'
'No, miss ... madam,' he corrected his error quickly and precisely. 'She left for the hospital right after she talked to you this morning.'
Rana nodded absently. 'Of course, of course, that's where she'd be. What hospital, Henson?'
'The Royal Alexander, madam.'
She put a shaking hand to her forehead, feeling suddenly drained of all energy. Looking about her, she was struck by the immensity and the stern emptiness of the house. Even when she had lived here as a child, this was how it had been—so very large and so very empty. She had always been lonely here and somehow today it housed an unnamed terror for her. The sun from the tall hall windows flooded the foyer with filtered gold light, the warmth the almost tangible touch of a heavy, suffocating hand. She stepped back towards the door, her heels echoing in the waxed hallway, feeling the desperate need to escape this place that was not home, that had never really ever been her home.
'Rana?' Heath's voice, concerned and questioning, halted her retreat. She turned to him, her eyes wide and her voice a pale, frightened whisper.
'Please, Heath, I want to go ... I ...' His hand slipped under her arm and he sought to guide her into the living room.
'Come and sit down. You're quite pale all of a sudden. I'll get you a drink of water ...'
But she pushed against him, moving again towards the door. 'No, please. I want to go to the hospital, Heath,' she said urgently. 'I must go now. We can take my car.' She flung open the door, only to come face to face with Dorothea Liscombe. 'Mother! We were just coming to see Daddy. We——' Her voice was cut in mid-sentence, as Mrs Lsicombe walked stiffly and silently past her, seemingly unaware of her presence. The older woman looked vacantly at Henson, and spoke in a lifeless, thin

monotone. 'I do wish Rana was here. Her father would have liked to have seen her. It was most irresponsible and unfair of her to go off with that man, especially at a time like this. I'll never understand the selfishness of young people, Henson. Do try to reach her on the phone again, will you.'

A wounded cry of disbelief and terror escaped Rana's lips, 'Mother, please, I'm here. What is it? Why are you talking like this?' She reached out to touch her mother's shoulder but was restrained by Heath.

'Easy, Rana. Don't startle her. She's had a shock of some sort—she's disorientated. Be still.' Heath did not try to move closer, but talked to Dorothea in a quiet, steady voice. 'Rana's here, Mrs Liscombe. Your daughter's home. She came to see her father. There's nothing to worry about. Wouldn't you like her to help you up to your room, fix you a warm drink? You look tired, I think you need a rest.'

His voice was lulling and deep, a steadying monotone that could not have startled Dorothea, but at the mention of Rana's name, her mother turned and quickly faced them. 'Rana? Where's Rana?' Her eyes unseeingly searched the faces before her, finally coming to rest on Heath's. 'You!' she cried accusingly. 'What are you doing in my home? You're not welcome here ... you'll never be welcome here. You took Rana from us, you took her and then you ...' she sobbed brokenly.

'Mother, come upstairs with me, please.' Rana's frightened voice pleaded.

'Rana's never disobeyed us, never!' Mrs Liscombe continued, 'But you—you turned her into a selfish, wilful and disobedient girl. A young tramp with no more thought ...'

Rana pushed past Heath, who stood fixed and staring at the distraught woman. 'Mother, don't do this, don't talk that way. I'm back and I don't understand why you're acting this way ...'

Her mother's eyes widened in recognition. 'You're a

selfish, evil girl, running off as you did with that Markland man ...' She was sobbing uncontrollably now. 'Your father died this afternoon, Rana, and you—you didn't even have the decency to come to him when he needed you.' She struck out blindly at Rana, slapping her forcibly across the face.

No one had expected her to do that, least of all Rana. A wordless moan escaped the girl's lips, as she sank limply to the floor, fighting against the blackness that threatened to engulf her. She reached out weakly for her husband. 'Heath ...' she whispered, and she felt him lift her easily into his arms, felt the security of his body holding hers, and heard his angry voice, cold and threatening, warning someone about something. And then she gave up the struggle for consciousness and slipped silently into the darkness.

The hours and days that followed were ones that Rana, later would find painful to remember, yet difficult to forget. She lived through them in a kind of a frozen numbness. Heath was with her continually, gentle, comforting, and strong, supporting her during the difficult time preceeding and during the funeral. Her mother had grudgingly apologised for what she had said to her, but the gulf that had always existed between them had been enlarged by Dorothea's actions and words, and also by the fact that now she took no pains to hide her aversion to Heath. It was obvious to Rana with each encounter that her mother's initial dislike of her husband had, for some illogical reason, unknown to her and unknown perhaps even to her mother, developed into an avid hatred. Heath seemed untouched by it, but it left Rana feeling bruised and weary. She longed to return to Clearwater, to the peace and solitude she and Heath shared there.

A few days after her father's funeral Rana, determined that it was best that she and Heath avoid more of her mother's bitter verbal thrusts, wandered downstairs in search of Heath, to suggest that they return to Clearwater in the morning. Hearing her mother's shrill voice raised in anger, Rana advanced towards the library. Her first instinct was to walk in and find out what was wrong now. But instead she hesitated at the door.

'I want you out of my house—now—you ... you murderer!' Dorothea Liscombe's eyes blazed with unconcealed hatred. 'I despise the very sight of you!'

'I know you weren't in favour of Rana's marriage to me, but what in God's name are you talking about now, Mrs Liscombe?' Heath's voice betrayed his weary frustration.

'It has nothing at all to do with your marriage to my daughter,' she responded cuttingly. 'She wanted you, so now she can have you. I don't happen to like it, but that's beside the point, obviously.'

Heath stood before her, controlled and taut in the face of her sudden attack. 'Then just what is the point, Mrs Liscombe?'

'I want you out of my house and I want you to leave now.'

'I think we'll be only too pleased to leave, I can assure you of that. But would you mind telling me what in the hell all this is about, if it has nothing to do with Rana's marriage to me?'

'You know damn well what it's about. You're a thief, and with all your conniving you've managed to murder my husband as well!'

Rana felt sure that they must have heard her sharp intake of breath as Dorothea uttered these words, but Heath remained towering threateningly over her mother, and Dorothea, crazed with hatred, leaned against the desk for support. Neither of them seemed to notice her move into the open doorway.

'I am not a thief, Mrs Liscombe—and how in God's name am I supposed to have murdered your husband?'

'You did—*you did*! You forced him to sign the business over to you, you forced him and left him with nothing.' Her voice broke. 'You took away everything he lived for and then he died. And you killed him!'

The tension in Heath's body was evident, a coiled spring, a deadly machine, ready to strike for survival. 'I bought Richard out, but I didn't force him to sign anything. And I paid him more than a fair price for a steadily failing business that's going to need a sizeable input of capital to bring it back to where it can begin to pay for itself again. He'd been worried for months, before I came along as a prospective buyer. Eli made the first contact between us. Ask him, Mrs Liscombe, go ahead and ask him, if you can't bring yourself to believe a Markland.' His last words were tinged with angry sarcasm.

'Oh yes—a Markland.' Mrs Liscombe spat the words, with obvious disdain. 'You're a Markland all right, just like your father and his father before him.'

'And what does that mean? God, woman, you're not making any sense at all.'

'You're just like them—hard and cruel, taking everything you can for yourselves, never once caring what you do to other people along the way.' Her eyes narrowed to pinpoints of venom. 'Why did you marry my daughter, Heath Markland? I mean, what was the real reason? Tell me the truth about that, at least. You knew we had plans for her, but you wanted to make your conquest of the Liscombes complete, didn't you? The business and the daughter too. How very convenient! A real step up the social ladder for the last of the Marklands.' She moved menacingly towards him. 'But wait, you may one day regret ever having laid eyes on her. She's not your kind and she never will be. She'll never be a Markland. Never! And your victory over the Liscombes will be like the taste of ashes in your mouth. A curse on you and all you count as your own, Heath Markland!'

Heath's face, strained and white, gave evidence that her words had at last struck home. 'You're ill, Mrs Liscombe. You're a sick woman. She's your own daughter, your flesh and blood, and you would hope that for her ...'

'Mother ...' Rana's thin, frightened voice issued from tense lips, sounded strangely small and pathetic in the midst of the heated passion of the argument. Rana had the strange and fleeting feeling that her mother was not surprised to see her standing there in the doorway, although Heath turned abruptly. 'How long have you been there, Rana?' he asked tightly. 'What have you heard?'

She put her hands to her head, trying desperately to make some sense of all that she had heard, trying to push away the cold foreboding that threatened to submerge her. 'I heard ...' she stammered, 'I heard mother accuse you of ...' she turned pleading eyes to Heath. 'What is she saying, Heath? What does she mean?'

He reached out to her and drew her close to him. But for once his touch did not soothe or make her feel safe. She struggled away from him. 'No! Tell me what she meant when she said ... that you murdered my father?'

'We'll talk about it when we're alone, Rana. Come on.' He would have led her from the room, but they were halted by Mrs Liscombe's angry, lashing words.

'You can't keep the truth from her, Heath. She'll know the truth of everything I've said.'

'You're a vicious, twisted woman, Mrs Liscombe,' he snarled. 'Leave her alone, what's between you and me—that's for us to settle. You've hurt her enough, I would say.'

'No, it's for her to know what her foolish, wilful ways have brought on us all.' She turned to Rana and the look in her eyes was not the love of a mother for her daughter but an almost twisted savagery and desire for vengeance. 'Your father died, Rana, because everything he had worked all his life to build and maintain was taken over, shortly after your marriage, by this man—your husband. He forced your father to sell to him, he took advantage of the fact that things had been going poorly for Richard lately and he stole the business, under the guise of a fair dealing.'

She went to the desk, gathered some papers in her shaking hand and marched to where Heath stood, his expression darkly unreadable. 'Deny it, Heath. Deny it ... if you can!' And she threw the papers into his face and they fell scattered on the floor at his feet.

He made no move to pick them up, but stood staring at her. 'You're mad, Mrs Liscombe, utterly mad,' he accused, his voice filled with disbelief. 'Either that, or you're one of the best damned actresses I've ever seen.'

'Deny it! Go ahead! You can't, can you? Oh no, there's no way that you can tell us that what I've said is not the truth,' she raged.

The next moments hung like lead between them, the miasma of fear and hatred covering them like a shroud. Rana turned slowly to look at her husband. 'Heath?' she questioned fearfully. 'Tell me.'

He sighed heavily, as if overcome by an intolerable weakness. 'What do you want me to tell you, Rana?' he asked dully. 'What must I say to you to wipe out the doubt I hear in your voice, the question that's evident in your eyes?' He reached out and swung her sharply towards him, his fingers biting into the tender flesh of her arms. 'Do you want me to tell you that I did buy your father's company? I did. Do you want me to tell you that I did it fairly, that I stole nothing from him? All right, I did. Did I kill your father?' He pushed her from him. 'Do you really,' he asked in a harsh whisper, 'expect me to answer a question that a man's wife should never have asked him in the first place?' He turned and walked to the door. 'I'll leave you two alone to deal with something you both obviously feel needs your attention.'

'Heath, please ...' Rana started to go to him, but he looked at her coldly, turned and walked away, his footsteps echoing in the tomblike silence of the house.

Torn between the desire to run after him, to stop him from leaving her in this way, to deal with the doubts and fears created by her mother's angry tirade, and the terrible need to know if her mother had spoken the truth, Rana put a hand on the back of the chair to support herself and her shaking legs. 'Oh, Mother, why? Why did you say all those terrible things to him? He's been kind to us, helped us through these dreadful days. He's . . .'

'He's done nothing that hasn't suited him, you foolish girl. He owns you now, just as he owns Liscombe Enterprises, so of course it would suit a Markland to take care of what's his. That's the way they all are, or were, at least. Now there's only Heath Markland left. God willing that'll be the end of them.'

Rana gasped in horror at the bitter implications of her mother's words. 'Dear God, Mother—do you know what you're saying? How could you hope such a thing? He's my husband, I love him . . . and he loves me . . .'

Her mother's eyes narrowed and she moved closer to her daughter. 'You don't know, do you? None of this makes any sense to you, does it?'

'No, not really. I know that you didn't want Heath and me to marry, that you wanted Boyd Dexter . . .' she stopped, realising for the first time that there was a deeper and far more serious reason for her mother's disapproval of her marriage to Heath. 'But that isn't it, is it, Mother? There's something else, isn't there?'

'Yes, there's something else, there's a great deal more, Rana, and I do think it's time you heard it.' Dorothea walked gravely to the library door, shut it, and turned the key. Turning to Rana, she said pointedly, 'Sit down, it's time you faced a few of the facts that will show you that people are not as honourable and ethical as you in your naïvety seem to believe, even at the age of twenty.'

A chill ran up Rana's spine, and suddenly she wanted only to rush from this room, to hear nothing of what her mother intended to say to her. Her mother began hesitantly, seemingly choosing her words with care. But not, Rana thought, because she didn't know what to say. The girl had the fleeting impression that her mother's words were rehearsed, well rehearsed. But this feeling was lost all too soon in the pain and confusion that resulted from Dorothea's revelations.

'The Marklands and the Liscombes are no strangers to one another, Rana.'

'I know that, Eli and Heath's grandfather were partners. Heath told me all about it. They were close friends and . . .'

'Don't interrupt,' Mrs Liscombe directed sharply, then seeing the look on her daughter's face, added, 'It's difficult enough to explain as it is.' Again Rana wondered about the truthfulness of this, for something about the flush of her mother's face and the brightness of her eyes seemed to indicate to Rana that the telling would not be difficult at all.

'Just as your grandfather and Sam Markland, Heath's grandfather, were partners, so were your father and Heath's father—Brent Markland. In fact, Liscombe Enterprises started as Liscombe-Markland Enterprises.'

'Oh no, Mother, Heath has never said anything about a connection between our families. Why, you and Daddy never once mentioned it. I would have known . . .'

'No, you wouldn't have known. There are a good many things that you wouldn't have known. In any case, this was before you were born.' Mrs Liscombe exhaled an exasperated breath. 'Oh, what's the use of breaking all this gently? Brent Markland, Heath's father, was an unscrupulous, cruel and dishonest man. For years, unknown to your father, he worked behind his back to take over the controlling interests in the company, did everything he could to discredit your father, to make him appear incompetent to the Board of Directors and the shareholders. But he didn't get away with it! Brent Markland was a thief and your father finally caught him at it. He caught him embezzling the company's funds. But your father was too soft and compassionate with him. I said then he should have sent the man to prison, given him just what he deserved, but no, your father would have none of that, so he bought out Brent's share in the company and the Marklands—Brent and his wife and two sons . . .'

'You mean Heath and Craig?'

'Yes, yes. Anyway, they quietly left Edmonton and moved back to the Peace River country, with no one but the Liscombes and the Marklands knowing the truth of why they left so suddenly. Brent went back to work with his father in his lumber business and did quite well with it, though God knows it couldn't have been honestly done.'

Mrs Liscombe lit a cigarette, her thin, well-manicured hands shaking slightly as she blew out the match. 'Damn, I seem to have misplaced my lighter, the one your father gave me . . .'

'But Mother, Heath and Craig were just boys when their parents died. Heath's grandfather brought them up.' Rana shook her head. 'Even if what you say is true, even if all this did happen, I can't really see what it has to do with Heath. He was a boy, he had nothing to do with it. He probably doesn't even know.'

'He has everything in the world to do with it. Bad blood, that's what runs through Heath Markland's veins, bad blood.'

'Mother, this is totally ridiculous! Do you really expect me to sit here and accept that outdated and unfounded piece of ancient folklore as support for what you say? Really, give me some credit for intelligence!'

'And give me some credit for the same thing, Rana! Heath and his brother had their father's ways, believe me. They proved it time and again. The first time Heath came here to the house a few weeks ago, and at your father's office, days before that, I saw it in him, the same cold ruthlessness that won't let him stop until he gets what he wants, whatever that might be. His brother Craig was wild, unmanageable, and he ended up killing himself.' She hesitated and then added, 'And I personally think that it was too bad Heath Markland didn't die with him in the same accident. Craig was wild, but Heath . . . he's evil. He has his father's dark, brooding evil in him.'

'Oh, God, Mother, how can you say that? Heath very nearly did die in that accident. He went through hell trying to save Craig.' She couldn't continue to argue with her mother. At this point she couldn't even think. She had no idea of the depth of her mother's hatred of Heath and could never, would never, accept her view of him. She knew, from her own experience, his gentleness, his kindness, as well as his strong will to live and face life as it was. There was a solid core of open honesty in Heath that she had not viewed in too many people, even in her young life. No, she could not accept her mother's accusations as valid and true.

'You still don't accept what I've told you, do you?'

'No, Mother. I don't believe what you say of him is true. I've seen none of these things in Heath.'

It was then that Mrs Liscombe picked up a book and some papers from her husband's desk and placed them in her daughter's hands. 'I suggest that you have a look at these, the terms of agreement of sale and the other documents. Then tell me if you think Heath Markland dealt fairly with your father. And if that doesn't convince you, read your father's diary entries during the last few months and see what your dear, devoted and honourable husband put him through. I doubt if you'll be able to argue with me after you've read these. Heath's responsibility for your father's death is clearly proved in these papers, as far as I'm concerned.' She walked quickly to the door, unlocked it, and left Rana alone with her warring emotions.

Hours later, tired and deeply disturbed by the things she had read, Rana walked slowly from the library across the silent hallway, and up the stairs to her bedroom, her footsteps silenced by the plush carpets. She rubbed her aching forehead, thinking desperately how much she really hated this house, this polished and well decorated institution. A 'Government House', Heath had called it. How she longed to escape it, wishing that she knew none of the things her mother had told her earlier in the evening, wishing fervently that she had read none of her father's tortured words in his diary. But she had heard and she had read, and the imprint of what she had discovered could not be erased. Heath had done all the things her mother had indicated. It was all there, no names in the diary, but a forthright indication of what it had cost her father to sell to Heath, and the pressure that had been applied to force him to do so. She quietly opened the door of the bedroom and slipped in without turning on the light. A deep voice filled the darkness. 'Well, Rana?'

Her eyes, accustomed now to the dimness in the room, saw Heath standing by the window, looking out over the city. 'I asked you a question,' he said quietly.

'Did you, Heath?' she responded coldly. 'I wasn't sure that it was a question.'

'Come here,' he said sharply, turning to face her.

'Heath, I'm tired. I want to go to bed. It's been a long day and . . .'

'I said come here, Rana.' His tone brooked no resistance.

Unwillingly, she walked over to the window. At first he didn't reach out to touch her but stood looking down at her, searching her face for the answer to his unspoken question. Then, slowly, he tilted her face to his, his fingers caressing the smoothness of her throat. 'Well, girl?' he asked huskily.

'I'm tired, Heath. I need to sleep,' she replied as evenly as she could.

His mouth found hers, parting her lips, seeking the sweetness of her response. Despite the clamouring of all her senses for fulfillment and union with this man, she forced herself to remain rigid in his embrace.

Abruptly he pulled away from her. 'So I have my answer, don't I?'

'I don't know what you mean,' she stammered.

'Don't you? Stop playing the innocent with me, Rana, my dear wife. You know full well what I mean. You've made your choice, whether you care to admit it or not. Your mother hasn't been able to accept the fact of our marriage and probably dearly hopes that it won't survive. I'd say she's made the first attempt at destroying it and . . .' he exhaled an angry breath, 'I'd also venture to say that she's succeeding. It's your job, as my wife, to trust me. I won't settle for less . . . I can't settle for less. But you don't trust me, Rana. You don't.'

'You're talking in riddles, Heath. You're not making any sense,' she protested feebly, while in her heart she knew that he spoke the truth. Her mother's revelations tonight had driven a barrier between them, but she could not gather the courage to say so. Not yet.

'Go to bed,' he muttered.

'Are you . . . are you coming?'

'Later.' And he turned back to the window.

For a moment she thought she detected in his voice a note of unbearable sadness, but she quickly decided that it must have been tiredness. 'Goodnight, then . . .' she whispered. But he did not respond.

Hours later Rana finally slept, although Heath had not come to her. And in the morning he was gone, having left a message with Henson to say he had business to attend to; 'something about a problem with an oil well, he said, madam', Henson had told her. He had expected to be back in two or three days, but it was nearly a week before he returned. When he did, it was as suddenly as he had left, arriving just before the evening meal and disappearing to his room with very little greeting for anyone. He was tired, unshaven, and decidedly not in a good mood.

Rana had spent a soul-searching week, fighting a desperate and losing battle with the demon her mother had unleashed. She loved Heath and always would, she knew this with a certainty. But it was not enough, and it could never compensate that she no longer trusted him and that she had finally come to believe that he was, in fact, responsible for her father's death. He himself had said he couldn't settle for less than her complete trust; she knew now that she wouldn't ask him to. Their marriage could never withstand the scars of her disbelief, so Rana had finally decided that, if they were going to be able to make a life for themselves, it would have to be apart from one another. Her mother had supported her decision to leave Heath and seek a divorce. Rana didn't know how to broach the subject with Heath, and his sudden reappearance, with no word of explanation concerning his whereabouts during the past week, did nothing to assuage her raw and hurt feelings.

They were in their room, changing for dinner, when Rana finally broke the strained silence between them. 'Well, I was beginning to wonder if you intended to come back at all?' Her tongue was sarcastic and cutting and it obviously had the desired effect. Heath stood still, his eyes narrowed, but when he spoke his voice betrayed no emotion.

'Why do you say that, Rana? You talk as if that was your preference.'

She turned from him and stared out of the window, the blackness of the night jewelled by the lights of the city, her reflection thrown back at her. 'Maybe it would have been easier if you hadn't,' she whispered.

'Speak up, Rana. I don't think I can have heard you correctly,' he said harshly.

'Yes, you did hear me!' Her voice filled with anger. 'I said that it would have probably been easier if you hadn't come back.'

'Easier in what way ... and for whom?' He was clearly struggling to keep his own anger in check as he pulled at his tie and flung it on the bed. He looked desperately tired, and despite everything she felt the urge to go to him and erase the lines of weariness from his face. 'You didn't answer me, Rana. I want to know what you meant.'

She shrugged and turned back to the window. 'Never mind, we can talk about it later. No use spoiling a good meal.'

He uttered an oath and gripped her by the arms, turning her roughly to face him. 'Damn you—I'm not one of your catty friends, Rana. I won't be dismissed by you until you can find a more convenient time to deal with me.' He shook her, frustration mingling with his fury. 'Don't you ever turn your back on me like that again, do you hear me?'

She struggled against his painful grip. 'You're hurting me! Let me go,' she said petulantly. He released her but gave her no chance to escape.

'I want to know what you meant by that remark, Rana.'

'I meant exactly what I said. It would have been easier if you hadn't come back here at all.' She spoke each word succinctly, as if trying to teach a child a lesson.

'Why?' he responded brusquely.

'Because ... because I've decided not to go back to Clearwater with you ...' she hesitated, seeing the menacing flash of anger in his eyes, but forced herself to continue. 'I made a mistake. I should never have married you ...' It was as if a dam had broken, releasing all her doubts and betrayal. 'I don't understand you and the way you live ... and think ... and the kinds of things you do. I'll never be able to. We just aren't the same kind of people, Heath, and if we stay together, we'll destroy each other. We made a terrible mistake and now we have to try ... I'm not going back with you, that's all. I'll see my lawyers and they'll contact you about divorce proceedings.' There, she'd said it. And now she waited, trembling for his response.

'Well, you certainly have everything planned, Rana.' Surprisingly, his voice was toneless, revealing nothing of his feelings. His face had become a mask, made fearful by the very fact that she could read nothing of the man there. 'Why? Or is that a superfluous question, my dear?'

'Why? What do you mean ... why? You know the answer to that.'

'No, I don't. I want to know why you've decided all this, all in the space of a few days. It sounds more like your mother's planning than yours.' His cold stare pinned her mercilessly, and no matter how much she wanted to, she could not look away.

'It's what I want. Mother has nothing to do with it.'

'You're a liar,' he rasped. 'She's used the days of my absence to her advantage and you, as usual, follow her directions like a child. For God's sake, Rana, grow up. See things, see people for what they are.'

'I do. Believe me I do,' she replied bitterly. 'I see what you are. I know what you did to my father. I know now what I am to you ... I'm part of the business deal, aren't I? Part of the property you've acquired from the Liscombes.' Tears threatened and she roughly wiped them away. 'And I won't be that! I won't!'

He stood before her, white lines etched around his mouth, a muscle twitching at the base of his throat. 'You believe that, don't you? You really do believe everything you've just said.'

'Yes! Yes ... every word. And I meant it when I said I wasn't going back to Clearwater with you.' She paused for a moment, then added, 'Maybe it would be better if you left here tonight.'

He reached savagely for her, grabbing her wrist with vicious strength. 'Now, I want you to listen to me. And hear me well, for I mean everything I'm about to say to you. First of all, I'm not leaving here tonight and when I do go, you'll be with me. You're my wife and you'll remain my wife.'

'You can't force me to go with you, to stay with you. You can't!' She tried to pull away from him, but he only tightened his hold and pulled her roughly back against him.

'Can't I? Surely a man as evil and depraved as I is capable of just about anything, my dear. *We* leave for Clearwater in the morning, after a "pleasant" family dinner tonight with your dear mother—during which, by the way, you will breathe nothing of your reasons for coming with me.'

'Oh? And what might they be?' she retorted.

'Very simple reasons indeed. If you want your mother to continue to live in the style to which she's accustomed, then you'll come with me. The other choice is obvious. Stay here with her and know that you'll both be seriously reduced in your style of living. This place will promptly be sold out from under you, for your father was a hair's breadth from bankruptcy—and I bought his business and hold options on all his property, this house included. As far as your mother is concerned, that would be a disgrace. Could she stand it, Rana? For that matter, could you?'

She stared at him incredulously. 'You wouldn't. You wouldn't do so foul a thing!'

'Wouldn't I, Rana? Answer that question as you've answered all the others. Look at how I dealt with your father, as your mother said. I have no scruples, no ethics, no honour when it comes to getting and keeping what's mine. You've already decided that. Well, now I'm proving it. Make up your mind, it's your decision.'

'I hate you ... I hate you, Heath Markland! I curse the day I married you ...'

'That's your choice, Rana ... but marry me you did.' He pulled her against him, his mouth roughly claiming hers, but she remained rigid and unresponding to his demands until at last he pushed her from him. 'That too is your choice, but I doubt if you'll be able to feign immunity to my touch for very long.'

She glared at him with utter disdain. 'How can you want to touch me at all, knowing what I feel about you?'

'A basic elemental need, my dear. You have it too, if you'd unthaw long enough to realise it. Would you rather I took my need elsewhere? That undoubtedly could be arranged.'

'You're ... you're barbaric, that's what you are!'

He laughed mirthlessly. 'Well, well ... unscrupulous, unethical, and now barbaric. A rather ominous combination, I would say. So don't push me, Rana, you know what I'll do.' He grabbed his jacket from the bed. 'Get dressed, we have an appearance to make downstairs in ten minutes, Mrs Markland. No use ruining a fine meal, as you say.' He turned and walked out of the bedroom, slamming the door behind him.

CHAPTER EIGHT

RANA leaned back in the chair, her eyes closed to the white glare of the afternoon sun. Her friend's soft voice picked up another strand of their relaxed conversation and Rana turned her attention to it.

'I was just saying to Jim last night how glad I am that you're here, Rana. Heath isn't the only lucky one ... I am too.'

Rana opened her eyes and looked at Beth Hinton, her gaze hidden behind dark glasses, as Beth continued, 'I've never really had a close woman friend to talk to and be with. But I do now, and I really do appreciate our friendship, Rana.'

'I do too, Beth. In many ways, you make my living here bearable,' Rana said sadly. Beth's quick and somewhat startled look told her that she had slipped and she spoke quickly to cover her error. 'What I mean to say is that with Heath away so much it would be unbearably lonely, but you and Jim make it ... well ...' she fumbled for the right words, '... easier, somehow.' Beth seemed to accept her explanation and Rana breathed a small sigh of relief; it was true, getting to know Beth and Jim Hinton had made living here with Heath bearable. But no one, under any circumstances, must know the truth of the basis of her marriage to Heath. And especially not Jim and Beth, who were, and had been for so many years, close friends of Heath's. They'd grown up together, gone to school together, and Heath had been the best man at their wedding. Now, in the months since her marriage to Heath, the Hintons had often been guests in their home and they in theirs. At first, just after her return to Clearwater from Edmonton two months ago, Rana had found it very difficult to be with them. They were people who knew Heath almost as well as they knew themselves and Rana feared that she would not be able to maintain the charade her husband had insisted upon. But her quiet, withdrawn attitude, her reticence in joining in their conversations, was accepted by them as a result of the recent loss of her father, and Heath had encouraged this viewpoint. Gradually, however, Rana was able to accept Jim and Beth Hinton as her friends as well, and she and Beth spent long hours together, talking and laughing, swimming and walking, and generally being comfortable together. As far as Rana was concerned, Beth and Jim noticed nothing unusual about her relationship with Heath, for it was a subject never touched upon by either of them, and Rana was only too pleased to leave it that way.

'How about a nice tall glass of iced-tea, Rana?' the other girl queried.

'Yes—that'd be lovely, I think.' She wiped the perspiration from her forehead. 'It's hotter today than it was yesterday, if that's possible.'

'Ummmm ...' Beth responded worriedly. 'It's hotter

all right, and if things go on much longer like this, we'll be sitting on a tinder box.'

Rana sat up and shifted her slight weight in the lounge chair. She had lost quite a bit of weight during the past weeks, but her skin now held a healthy golden glow that came from living more in the outdoors than she ever had in her life.

'Sit still, Rana. I can get the tea. It was my idea in the first place,' offered Beth.

'Don't be silly. Relax. I need to move around or I'll fall asleep on the spot. I'll be back in a minute.' Rana smiled and went indoors, the screen door slamming in the silence of the summer afternoon, a silence punctuated by the lazy drone of insects in the sweltering heat. It was cooler inside the house than out and it took a moment for her eyes to grow accustomed to the relative darkness of the interior. The white glare of the sunlight still imprinted itself before her eyes and for an instant she felt dizzy, as if she had got up too quickly. Damn this heat, she thought, as she made her way to the kitchen. She took the cold pitcher of tea from the refrigerator, relishing the frosted coolness in her slim hands. Two months, she thought, it had only been two months since her father's death and their subsequent return to Clearwater. To her it seemed more like two years, when in fact it had only been two long and bitter months.

In the beginning she didn't really think that Heath would make her stay. She couldn't believe that, knowing the truth of her feelings for him, he would want her with him. But he was relentless in his demands on her—she was his wife legally and he had no intention of letting her go. As far as he was concerned, she was his property, another business acquisition. How she hated him for viewing her as such, just as she hated herself for the way her treacherous body betrayed herself to him each and every time he came to her. They shared the same bed, they lived together physically, and while their physical relationship gave something to both of them, never would he ever again hear her say that she loved him. She vowed to herself that she would never again give him that. Once she had loved him, probably from the first moment of their first meeting and certainly, she acknowledged to herself that it was love that she felt for her husband at the time of their first coming together; their union had blazed with all the passion and heat of a searing white fire. But all that changed when she learned the dreadful secret of her husband's involvement in her father's death. That and the fact that he refused to let her go, using the direst of threats to keep her with him had destroyed her love for him and served to harden her heart against him.

No, it was no longer love that burned within her, but a hatred that burned as brilliantly and with a heat as startlingly fierce as the love she once bore for him. And she would never let him forget it. She would punish him, every moment of their existence, together with the knowledge that he would never gain her forgiveness for what he had done to her father and for what he now forced upon her—a loveless marriage, a marriage based on hatred and mistrust. She would play her role effectively in front of any guests or friends, but he would never be mistaken about the truth of her feelings for him when they were alone. Never.

Not that it would matter that much to him anyway, she told herself bitterly. If anything, it would only be his pride that would be injured, for she was under no illusions that he was vulnerable to her feelings towards him. He didn't love her, he had never loved her, he had merely seen something he had wanted and had astutely been able to obtain it. Their physical relationship served to meet his 'elemental' needs, as he had put it those two long months ago, but she knew that he would never let her matter enough to be hurt by her. She doubted if, in fact, anyone had ever mattered that much to Heath Markland, except perhaps his brother Craig.

Beth's voice, calling from the verandah, brought her

back from her secret thoughts. 'Are you all right in there, Rana? You haven't fainted from the heat, have you?'

'No. I'll be right with you.' She poured the tea, half filled the glasses with crushed ice, cut a few wedges of lemon, and walked back through to the verandah. 'Here we are, Beth. Sorry I took so long,' she smiled, 'but I guess I'm a daydreamer from way back.'

Beth took the glass Rana held out to her and teased, 'Daydreaming about Heath, eh?'

Rana looked up sharply, but knew instinctively that Beth had only been referring to the normal daydreams any newlywed young woman would have.

'When's Heath due home this time?' Beth went on innocently.

Rana sat down on the lounger and drank deeply of the cold tea. 'Oh, tomorrow some time, I guess. He didn't say exactly when.'

'Well, he'll probably call you tonight some time and let you know for sure.'

'No. He'll be here when he gets here.' How could she explain that Heath refused to account to her or anyone about his time or his whereabouts? Often now he would mention only on his way out the door that he wouldn't be back for two or three days. Even then he didn't always tell her where he was going. Often too, late at night, she would awaken to the drone of his airplane, flying low over the lake. She refused to admit it, even to herself, but the sound of his plane, signalling his return, also brought with it a measure of relief; he had returned safely. For one of the images she was never able to exorcise from her mind was the picture of Heath and his brother, struggling against almost immeasurable physical odds after the plane crash that proved fatal for Craig Markland; it was a recurring nightmare when Heath was away. She brushed this from her mind quickly as she realised that Beth was asking her something.

'Goodness, Rana, but you seem to be a million miles away this afternoon!'

'I know, I'm sorry I'm such bad company, but I think the heat has got to me at last. I can't seem to keep my mind on anything today. Surely this can't go on for much longer.'

'I don't know.' Beth shook her head, not trying to disguise the fact that she was truly worried about the unbroken spell of hot, dry weather that had already lasted nearly five weeks. 'Jim and Heath seem to think we're in for it this time. It could mean real trouble for Heath if it doesn't break soon.'

'Nothing that the mighty Heath Markland won't be able to handle, I'm sure,' replied Rana.

This time, she was unable to disguise the sarcasm that was evident in her voice. Beth looked at her searchingly. 'What's the matter, Rana? That's twice this afternoon you've said something like that. Is the fact that Heath's away so much lately starting to get to you?'

'No ... yes ... I don't know,' Rana murmured, annoyed that Beth had noticed her other comment; she must be more careful, she told herself angrily. 'Look, it's really just the heat.'

Beth didn't look at her, but said seriously, 'You can't blame everything on the weather, Rana. There's nothing to be ashamed of if you're feeling lonely. It takes some getting used to, I imagine. You come from a completely different background from Heath's. Are you bothered being left alone so much, being just married and all?'

'I don't know what it is exactly, Beth,' Rana lied, wanting the other girl to drop the subject, and cursing herself for making the stupid slip in the first place. 'I guess it may be the adjustment to living with someone, as well.' She hesitated and then added with false lightness, 'Oh, who knows what it is, Beth. Besides, it's nothing serious, so don't start worrying about me.'

Beth leaned forward. 'I do worry about you. Sometimes you seem so strained, as though you have something on your mind, something that's bothering you. I don't mean to push it or invade your privacy, but if there's something wrong and you'd like to talk about it, I'd like to listen. I'm your friend, Rana, and I know it must be terribly lonely out here with Heath away so much.' She assumed a mockingly thunderous frown. 'Darn that man, anyway. He finally finds a woman like you to settle down with and do you think he can stay home? Lord, but he's getting his brother's wandering ways.'

'You mean Craig?'

'Yes. Did you know him, Rana?'

'No, I didn't, but Heath's told me all about him, and about the accident that killed him.'

'Yes, that was a hard thing for Heath to live with, I can tell you. They were like this, all the time they were growing up together.' She crossed her fingers to symbolise the closeness of the two Marklands. 'But still they were so different. Craig could never stay still for long, but Heath—well, he was calmer, quieter, and held more to himself somehow.' Beth continued to talk, almost forgetting Rana's presence. 'He had a rough time coming back to us all after what happened to Craig. It seemed to take all the spirit out of him and he kept totally to himself for a long while. He seemed harder and colder than the Heath we knew before. Then, after a while, he came round, but he was never quite the same.' She smiled happily, 'Not until he met you, anyway. Then the Heath we used to know surfaced again.' Beth reached out and touched Rana's hand. 'You've been good for him, Rana. He needed someone like you ... so don't ever think, because he works so hard and is away so much, that ... well, you know what I mean. He loves you, that's obvious. It's just a hard time in the lumbering business, I guess. He doesn't go so often because he wants to, I'm sure.'

Rana fought a rising desire to put her hands to her ears and scream at Beth to curb the flow of her words. Dear God, if she only knew the truth of what Rana meant to Heath. If only Beth knew how foolish and how ironically hollow her words sounded in the face of what actually existed between Rana and her husband. Perhaps Heath once was as Beth had described him, and perhaps he had changed after his brother's death; but the man of whom Beth now spoke was as foreign to Rana as she was sure he was foreign to reality. As far as Rana was concerned, he simply did not exist. Beth was remembering a childhood friend; a friend long since gone.

'Well, what do you think?'

Rana started. 'I'm sorry. I've done it again. What were you saying?'

'I was asking you to come home with me for supper and spend the night with us. Jim has a meeting tonight and won't be in until late, so we could maybe take in a movie or something. After all, Rexton's theatre is one of the few places, if not the only place, in town that has air-conditioning.' Beth laughed heartily. 'It's always been a bit of a joke, air-conditioning up here, but it'd be a pleasure to be there tonight, I can tell you. What do you say, Rana? Will you come back to Rexton with me?'

Rana hesitated. 'I don't think so, Beth. Heath could get back tonight. I'm not sure just when he . . .'

'You said yourself that he probably won't get back till tomorrow. So leave him a note just in case he gets home tonight and come stay with us. We'd love to have you, really we would.'

Suddenly Rana realised that she didn't want to be alone any more. She had spent too many long, lonely nights here at Clearwater during the past two months and tonight she wanted to be with people who could make her forget her unhappiness, even if only for a few hours. She stood up quickly. 'All right, Beth, I will come with you,' she said decisively. 'In fact, it's probably just what I need, to pull me up out of this depression that's settled in on me.' She smiled mischievously and added, 'Which is probably caused by the heat and nothing else, by the way.'

*

They enjoyed a light supper, went to a movie, and when Jim came home from his meeting the three of them sat in the kitchen, talking late into the night, sharing a comradeship that was easy and comfortable. For a while the ghosts of loneliness that haunted Rana were banished. Finally she could stay awake no longer. 'Look, guys, I hate to kill a good party, but I've got to go to bed. I'm starting to fall asleep sitting here.'

'Sure, Rana,' Jim said, and looked at Beth. 'The spare room's ready, isn't it, dear?'

'Everything's set out for you. If you don't mind, Jim and I are going to stay here for a while and just chat. Heath isn't the only one who's been on the go lately. This doctor of mine burns his candle at both ends and the middle too sometimes.'

'Heavens no, I don't mind. I'll see you both in the morning. And ...' Rana hesitated, '... thanks for everything. I did need to get away tonight. You are, both of you, such good friends.' She turned, half-embarrassed, and ran quickly up the stairs, the echo of their cheerful 'goodnight' following behind her.

Despite her tiredness, sleep did not claim her immediately. She lay, alone in the darkness, wondering where Heath was, and what he was doing. She could not explain the terrible ache, the longing she had for the sight of him. He'd been away for nearly a week now, and there had been no word from him. She thought of Beth and Jim and suddenly, painfully, found herself wishing desperately for the kind of relationship they so obviously shared. Perhaps, after all, it had not been wise to stay with them, when it only served to make the stark reality of her own situation more difficult.

She crushed a sob, turning her face into her pillow. You're a fool, Rana Markland, if you shed even a single tear for that man, she admonished herself. He doesn't deserve it. He wants nothing from you—nothing but the physical claims he has a legal right to make on you as his wife, she thought bitterly. Finally, a troubled sleep claimed her.

Hours later, or what seemed like hours, a fierce pounding on the back door made her sit bolt upright in bed. Someone needed Jim. That was her first thought as she turned on the light beside her bed and grabbed her housecoat, glancing at the clock as she made for the door. It was barely an hour since she had come to bed, she realised. She was midway down the stairs when the door opened and the voice she heard made her grasp at the varnished smoothness of the banister.

'Where is she, Jim?' Heath demanded, in tones as cold and hard as steel.

'Good heavens, man—what's wrong with you? If you don't mind my using a cliché, you look as if you've seen a ghost. Come in. Come in—don't just stand there making all this racket—it's bound to wake the neighbours.' He moved back to allow Heath to come into the kitchen. From the darkness on the stairs, Rana could see Heath's taut and angry stance; he looked tired and strained, but she could not bring herself to go to him.

'Damn your neighbours, Jim. And ...' he turned angrily on his friend, 'Damn you for interfering with my personal life! Now where is she?'

'I presume you mean Rana?' Jim enquired calmly. 'And if you do, she's upstairs in the guest room, sleeping, or at least she was an hour ago ... before you decided to come charging in here like a stampeding herd and probably woke her up, along with half the neighbourhood, I might add.'

'Don't play games with me, Jim. You've known me long enough to realise that I don't appreciate it. Go get her. I'm taking her home ... now!'

'Hold on, Heath. What's this all about?'

Heath moved forward and for an instant Rana thought that he meant to strike Jim. But then, as if fighting to hold the remnants of his control, he drew back. 'You have no right to bring her here. She had no right to come running to you with our problems,' he rasped. 'She's my wife and we'll settle any differences between us. That's the way it is. There'll be no outside interference. Now get her down here.' This time he intended his movements to be threatening. 'I want to see her now.'

Jim didn't move. 'Heath Markland, you can believe me or not, but I haven't the faintest idea what you're so upset about. We both know it would be a very simple matter indeed if you wanted to start, and consequently win, a physical debate with me. But by God, you'll have to walk over me to get to that girl with you acting the way you are right now.' He paused. 'I'm not sure it's safe for her to go back to Clearwater with you.'

'Get out of my way, or by God, I will walk over you!'

'And will you walk over me too, Heath? Because you'll have to. Until we get an explanation for this madness and until you calm down, Rana's going nowhere with you.' Beth's steady voice sounded behind Rana, and she walked calmly past the frightened girl, who still held fast to the banister. When Heath turned his attention to Beth, he saw Rana standing there. He moved to the bottom of the stairs, and would have started up after her, had Beth not remained firmly blocking his way. He issued a cold order. 'Get dressed, Rana. You're coming home with me.'

'No, Heath,' directed Beth. 'Jim's already told you that she's not coming with you ... not this way. And ...' she drew herself up in front of him, defying the fierceness of his intentions, 'don't try to threaten me. You never could and you can't now. Rana was lonely and depressed at Clearwater this afternoon, so I persuaded her to come here for supper, then we took in a movie. She went to bed about an hour ago and then you came busting in here, acting like the proverbial madman. I've accounted to you for our "innocent" behaviour of this evening and now I think that we deserve your explanation.' She paused, but not long enough to let him speak. 'Good

God, Heath, you're acting like a wronged and jealous husband. What did you think, that she'd left you or something? Didn't you get her note?'

Heath swung abruptly away, and rigidly stood with his back to them all, unresponding.

'So that's it,' Beth breathed in astonishment, 'that's what's wrong with you. You thought that Rana ...' She walked over to Heath and put a hand on his shoulder. 'Heath, please. I'm sorry that I ...'

Heath turned slowly to look at her, the look of unmasked pain a fleeting shadow in his dark eyes. 'Leave it alone, Beth,' he said huskily. 'For God's sake, just leave it alone.' He looked beyond her at Rana, who stood staring at him, her housecoat wrapped tightly around her slim and shaking body.

'There was no note ... was there, Rana?' he said dully. She shook her head. 'I'll wait for you in the jeep. We'll come back in the morning to get your car.'

Jim moved to prevent his retreat. 'Please, Heath. Don't go like this.'

'I won't hurt her, Jim. You have no worry in that quarter,' Heath said sadly, almost lifelessly.

'Why don't you stay here tonight?' Beth begged.

Heath's only response was to shake his head and walk silently from the house.

The drive back to Clearwater was achieved in total silence, and for Rana, in total discomfort. Heath was withdrawn and uncommunicative, never once turning to look at her. She had not left a note, purposely, she realised now, hoping somehow deep within her that Heath would come and find her gone, hoping that he would believe that she had left him. This afternoon she had relished the thought of making him angry by her unexplained departure, but she had not expected such a violent and desperate reaction, and had been totally unprepared for the look of tortured agony that had been evident in his eyes at Beth and Jim's. So now she struggled to comprehend his reaction, trying to brush aside the nagging feeling of guilt and despair it had created.

Heath parked the jeep in front of the verandah, took out her overnight bag and stood back to let her enter the house before him. Once again she felt like a prisoner re-entering her cell, after a brief and futile attempt at freedom. He didn't bother to turn on the lights but moved unerringly through the darkness to their bedroom. Rana followed in silence. Damn him, she thought. Why should I come slinking back here at three in the morning, feeling guilty, as though I've done something wrong? He's the one who's been gone for nearly a week, with no word to tell me that he's all right or when he'd be coming back. He's the one who made a fool of himself tonight, made our relationship public knowledge; she didn't know how she would ever face Beth and Jim again. And it was all Heath's fault. No amount of pretence on her part now would hide the truth from their friends.

In the bedroom he stood for a long time with his back to her, looking out at the lake. The moon was full and round, a cold ball of white fire, floating in the black velvet sky. The only sounds in the still night air were the gentle lapping of the lake against the shore and the lonely hooting of an owl. The sweet smell of the forest wafted through the open patio doors.

Rana wanted to ignore him, to turn her back on him and go to sleep. But the sight of him standing there alone against the night made it impossible. She walked over to the patio and reached out, tentatively touching him on the arm. He neither stiffened nor withdrew, but seemed imune to her touch. Only his white-knuckled grip on the railing belied her assumption of his unawareness of her presence. That, and haunted pain that glistened in his eyes when he turned to look at her from the far, untouchable depths of his own private hell. God, she thought desperately, I did this to him?

'Heath . . .' she whispered, not really knowing what she

wanted to say, but wanting only to bring him back, to make some kind of contact.

He looked back at the lake, absorbed in its still, glass-like surface that reflected the splash of white light from the moon. Then he spoke, quietly, as if from a very great distance. 'You know, Rana, I always thought that no matter what happened to me out there in the world of other men, no matter what madness overtook me and threatened my survival as the kind of man I was and wanted to be ... no matter what happened, however evil and destructive, and difficult to bear ... that Clearwater was my refuge, would always be my salvation. But I was wrong ... as I found out tonight.' He looked at her intently. 'From some things there is no refuge and no haven. You, my dear wife, have shown me that. You ... have managed to take even Clearwater from me. There's no peace ... even here.'

Suddenly he reached out and seized her, pulling her roughly against him, the heat of his body touching her, searing her, stirring a desire that met and equalled his. He lifted her easily in his arms and carried her to the bed, his heart beating a mad passionate rhythm. The fire of their need for one another consumed them, destroyed their awareness of themselves as two separate persons. They made love, and became one, with a desperation that neither of them understood. Afterwards, they lay close together, Rana cradled in Heath's arms, both trying to elude the separation that they knew must inevitably come.

'Damn you, Rana, you're a witch woman,' Heath said huskily, his mouth probing and plundering her body, which for him now held no secrets. 'You make my life a hell, and still I can't get enough of you. You're my woman, Rana, and I'll never let you go. I want you as I've wanted none other ...'

She pulled herself away from him, the sting of his words cutting through the ecstasy of their lovemaking, tearing asunder the slender thread of their union, shattering their closeness like the fragile crystal thing it was. 'And damn you, Heath Markland!' She flung the words at him, cruelly striking out to wound him in return. 'It always comes to that, doesn't it? I'm your property, your woman, part of the Liscombe takeover. Well, make no mistake, I hate you, and that's all you'll ever get from me! I hate you, do you understand?'

His eyes blazed again with angry fire as he seized her by the wrists and pulled her back against the length of him, forcing her to touch his face and the hard muscles of his chest; to feel his thighs against hers. 'Feel me, Rana. Touch me,' he demanded. 'I'm the man that you came to willingly. I'm the man who fills you with the fire of life. Tell me that the life we give to each other is based on hatred. You want and need me as I want and need you. I'll never believe that it's hatred that joins us so completely. Never.'

Driven by her desire to hurt him, to break away from the awesome power he held over her, to make him pay for his part in her father's death; driven too by her own self-loathing for not having the strength to leave him despite his threats, she recklessly flung her next words at him. 'Don't be a fool, Heath! You explained it all so well yourself once, months ago. It's plain "elemental" need, my dearest, nothing more. Women have it too, in case you haven't noticed.' Spitefully she added, 'And, to extend your previous offer ... if you prefer that I fulfill my needs elsewhere, I'm sure that could also be arranged.'

His face paled and he drew a sharp breath. His fingers caressed the smooth whiteness of her throat. 'Sometimes I think you could drive me ... to kill ... Rana,' he breathed harshly. Fear of the restrained violence of this man, her husband, whom at this moment she hardly recognised, surged within her. 'No other man will ever touch you, I promise you that. Like it or not, you'll soon have to give in to the reality of the fact that you're *mine*, Rana.'

'And you, Heath Markland,' she whispered fiercely, daring to defy his anger, 'you might as well face the fact that what you truly want of me, you will never have. I do hate you, and that will never change.'

CHAPTER NINE

THE weather remained hot and dry, with no relief in sight. Heath began work at the lumber camp south of Clearwater, leaving at sunrise each morning and returning just before dark. Each day Rana expected him to fly from Clearwater on one of his longer trips, but she soon realised that he intended, at least for the time being, to stay close to home. Generally they saw very little of one another with Heath working hard and long hours, and the time they did spend together was filled with strained silences.

Late one afternoon Rana was in the kitchen preparing supper, when she heard the screen door open and then slam shut. Maybe it was Beth—she hadn't seen her friend since the flare-up at their house nearly two weeks ago. 'Beth?' she called. 'Is that you? I'm out here in the kitchen. Come on through.'

She missed her times with Beth, and although she had no intention of discussing what had happened between herself and Heath, she still valued and intended to maintain her friendship with the other woman. But it was not Beth who came to stand in the doorway.

'Were you expecting Beth today?' Heath's quiet voice questioned her. Rana turned, startled at the sound of his voice, surprised to see him home so early.

'No ... not really,' she replied coolly. 'But I didn't expect you to be home so early and no one else ever comes out here.'

'Ummm ...' he responded absently. 'Wasn't that Bill Stewart I just saw leaving?'

She looked at him, puzzled by his question. 'What?'

'I wondered if Bill Stewart was here looking for me. I saw his jeep pull out of our road as I rounded the bend. I'm sure it was him.'

'No ... no one's been here at all today. No one ...' She frowned wondering why anyone would come as far as the road and then decide not to come in.

'Never mind,' he said evenly, 'if he wants to see me, he'll come back.' He wandered over to the refrigerator and took out a cold beer.

'Do you want an early supper?'

'It doesn't matter. Whatever suits you.' He wiped his forehead with the sleeve of his shirt. 'Well, it's starting,' he drawled.

She looked up at him, seeing the lines of tiredness etched into his face, his shoulders weary with the labour of long hours in the heat. She put down the paring knife and dumped the potato peelings into the compost bucket. 'What's starting?'

'The fires. We had two outbreaks today. Caught them both, but that was an accident in itself. We're for it, I'm afraid. We need rain desperately if it's to be avoided, but there's none in sight.'

'Why are you home so early?' she asked, as if she hadn't heard a word he'd said. He looked at her sharply, gauging the intent of her question. She realised suddenly how he'd taken her question and stammered an explanation. 'No ... I didn't mean ... I was just wondering why ...'

'Never mind it, Rana.' He threw the empty beer can into the garbage. 'I know what you meant,' he replied bitterly.

'No, you don't,' she said, her voice revealing her own tired frustration. 'I didn't mean anything by it, honestly.'

'Okay. Okay, just let's drop it. It's too damned hot to argue and I'm too tired.' He unbuttoned his sweat-stained shirt, took it off, and flung it into the clothes hamper. Rana looked at the corded muscles of his bronzed back, noticing how he'd lost weight. He's worn out, working night and day, she thought, longing to go to him and hold him, to ease away the ache of weariness that filled his body.

'Would you . . .' she began, then hesitated.

'Would I what?' he asked absently as he made his way to the door.

'Would you like to go for a swim before supper?'

He threw a sharp look at her and then stopped. 'Do you mean alone—or with you?'

'I mean with me. It's so hot. It would do us both good, I think.'

He nodded. 'Yes, it might at that.'

'I'll just take a minute to get changed.'

He laughed. 'And here we have Rana Markland, Miss Modesty, 1979.' He reached out and softly touched the smooth skin of her face. 'And what are you going to hide from me, sweet Rana, that I don't already know as well as my own heart? I know every inch of you, girl.'

Blushing, she pulled away from him, but his gentle voice pursued her. 'You're amazing, do you know that? We've been married four months now and you still blush for me . . . you're still shy.' She looked back at him, where he stood leaning lazily against the door frame, a light smile flickering on his lips. 'You enchant me, you really do—when you're not driving me to distraction, girl.'

He was swimming a fair distance off shore when she walked down to the wharf. The sun beat mercilessly down on her back and the sharp roughness of the grass scratched her feet. Everything was parched and withering in the dryness . . . surely the weather would break soon. She stood at the end of the wharf, watching Heath's strong body slice powerfully through the water. Watching him like this, so much a part of the world he and his family had carved out of the wilderness, she realised, ironically, that her feelings for him were anything but hostile. She did love him. No matter how she fought him and his control over her, she knew that she still loved this man, that she had never stopped loving him. If only, her heart ached as the thought painfully brushed her mind, if only he truly loved her.

They swam for nearly an hour, not playfully but strenuously, both of them enjoying the exhilaration, the feeling of power that the cool, clear water released in their bodies. They were tired and breathless when they climbed out and collapsed on the wharf. As they lay side by side on the warm wooden planks, the heat drying their tanned skins, Rana almost gave herself up to the fantasy that all was well between them, that their marriage was one of love.

'Rana?' Heath whispered into the silence. 'Are you asleep?'

'No.'

Turning over on to his stomach, he came close to her, his body touching hers. His grey eyes asked the same unaltered question. She turned her face from the closeness of his, fearful of the look in his eyes, a look that she did not entirely understand.

'Look at me, Rana ... we have to talk.' His voice held an urgency she had not heard before.

'What about?'

'I want to ask you something. Something that's important to both of us.'

She held her breath, thinking for a blinding moment that he had finally decided to release her, to let her leave Clearwater. She held her breath.

'I've been thinking, wondering ... if maybe it might not be a good thing for both of us if ... if we had a child.'

She stared at him, unable to speak.

'A child might help us resolve our problems ... might bring us together. If we could have a child, a tangible result of our love, then ...'

'Our love!' She leapt to her feet. 'A tangible result of our love, did you say? You must be mad! We share a bed, Heath, and you exercise your legal prerogative, but dear God, it's not love we share.'

He reached out and grabbed her by the wrist, wrenching her brutally to a halt when she would have run from him. Anger blazed in his eyes, and for a brief moment Rana thought she glimpsed raw pain and a plea for relief from some intolerable burden.

He eased his grip on her wrist but did not release her. 'Can't you understand, Rana? I love you. And I know of no other word for it.'

'Well, I do, damn you. It's called pride of ownership where I come from. Not love.' How dare he claim to love her, he who had never loved her?

He dropped her hand, the fire and anger fading from his eyes, to be replaced by the same look she had seen moments before but still did not understand. 'Goddamn you, Rana,' he groaned. 'What do you want from me? What in the name of heaven does it take to show you that I'm telling the truth?'

'Nothing! Nothing! But you can't seem to accept that. I don't want your child, Heath. I want to go, to leave Clearwater. I want to be free of you and our marriage. Let me go, Heath, it's the only way. Please ...' she sobbed, 'just let me go.'

He turned from her and looked out over the lake, the sun throwing its flaming reflections across the water like an arm of gold. 'I can't, Rana,' he rasped, 'God help me, but I can't let you go.'

Days melted into weeks and Heath seemed to withdraw further into himself, even though their visits to Beth and Jim resumed sporadically, and sometimes Rana went with him to the lumber camps. He worked harder than ever, coming to bed each night long after Rana; he slept poorly, fitfully, haunted by dreams of images he never mentioned or discussed with her. He did not speak again of his desire for a child, but she often caught him watching her, and thought at times that she saw in his eyes a look of unguarded agony.

Gradually, almost unconsciously at first, questions began to arise in her mind that for months she had refused to even consider. Heath worked hard, never avoiding his share of the strenuous physical labour at the camps. He was firm, straightforward, and fair with the men who worked for him, and he seemed to be greatly respected by them. These observations about him and his relationships with his workers and his friends ... all these things bespoke, not of the kind of man her mother had convinced her he was, but one of integrity, honour, and honest caring. Could she have misjudged this man, regardless of the evidence her mother had so flagrantly and cruelly presented to her?

But despite these doubts and questions, and despite her shy attempts to draw him out of himself, to broach her thoughts and feelings and fears—he remained cold and unapproachable, keeping her with him when he visited the camps but leaving her suddenly and often with no word of explanation and no indication of the time of his return.

Just before dusk one evening of a particularly hot day, when he had gone off alone at dawn, she heard slow plodding footsteps on the front verandah. He sounded very tired; it was not his usual firm step.

'Heath?' she called out, pushing open the front door and going out on to the verandah to meet him. But it was not Heath's face that loomed menacingly in front of her. She jumped back, startled by Bill Stewart's sudden and unexpected appearance, 'Oh, it's you.' She looked nervously beyond him for a sign of Heath, all of a sudden feeling chilled and frightened by the silence and the loneliness, and wishing fervently that Heath would come home. Where was he? she thought frantically. Her fear must have been evident to Bill Stewart.

'I've seen you around the camp with your husband

quite a bit lately, Mrs Markland. Still and all, he aint' around home all that much, is he now?' He watched her closely through squinted eyes. 'Still the lost city girl, feeling lonely way out here in the bush?'

'No ... no ... of course not!' she stammered. 'I'm quite accustomed to it here now.'

He leaned insolently against the side of the house. 'Aren't you going to invite me in, Rana? I can call you Rana, can't I, seeing as how we're all alone and the bossman's not here.' The smell of liquor lingered on his breath and fear rose within her as he leered at her.

'I think you'd better go, Mr Stewart. My husband will be here any minute now. He won't like it if ...'

He cut her off, a rough hand tightly grabbing her slim wrist. 'He won't like it, eh? It seems to me that a man who leaves a beautiful woman like you alone as much as he does must have someone else that interests him, so he really wouldn't mind so much at all if you and I got to know each other ... a little better.' His eyes narrowed threateningly. 'Go ahead, invite me in—Mrs Markland.'

Panic welled within her as she vainly tried to wrench free of his ironlike grip. 'Let go! You're hurting me! I want you to leave immediately ...' her voice faltered. 'Please, just leave me alone ...'

'It don't have to be unpleasant, Mrs Markland. Our friendship can be real enjoyable to both of us.' He released her wrist and raised his arms in a gesture designed to emphasise his words. 'It's up to you, Mrs Markland.'

In a flash, she seized the slim opportunity to get away from him. She turned and ran down the steps and across the lawn, not thinking of where she was going, wanting only to escape. Her heart thudded madly as the lake loomed and tilted with the rhythm of her terrified and erratic runing. The canoe. Maybe she could make it to the canoe.

Then he had her, his hand reaching out and seizing her long hair, wrenching her painfully to a stop and flinging her to the ground. She struggled and wrestled with him, but he defeated her by sheer weight alone. His mouth came down on hers, bruising, crushing, harsh. Tears of shame and revulsion filled her eyes.

'Please don't ... please don't touch me ... Heath! Heath ... help me ... Oh God, help me ...' Her desperate screams pierced the still air.

Suddenly a deep voice, tight and strained with controlled rage, halted Stewart's attack. 'Get away from her. Now!' Heath stood towering above them both, the threat of murder unmasked in his eyes. Weeping uncontrollably and unable to look at either of them, Rana lay shivering in the grass. Stewart scrambled to his feet, offering no excuse or apology and by appearances, readying himself for a fight.

'No, not here, Stewart. Go to the camp and pack your things. You're finished. We'll settle what's between us there.' Distraught as she was, Rana sensed heavy footsteps receding across the lawn. Then Heath knelt and gathered her trembling body into his arms and carried her into the house. He placed her gently on the bed. 'I'll draw a hot bath, it'll help you relax.'

She held tightly to his hand. 'No ... no ... please don't leave me. I want ... you ... to stay with me.' Tears again flooded her eyes. 'Hold me, please. Just hold me ...'

'Oh, my God, Rana——' he whispered hoarsely, drawing her against his chest and gently coming to lie beside her. They lay together for a long time, not talking, Heath holding her close, calming her, soothing her, and gently rocking her until her body relaxed against him. The shadows of dusk lengthened and deepened into darkness.

'Why, Heath? Why did he do it?' she asked, shuddering as fearful images again clouded her mind. 'I just don't understand.'

'It's all right, girl, you're safe now. I'll never pretend to be able to understand men like Bill Stewart. I guess they think they can take what they want when they want it.'

'That's barbaric ... it's insane. I'm your wife! He knows that, how could he dare to ...'

'Rana, please don't get upset again. It won't happen again.' His voice hardened. 'I promise you that. You rest for a while. I have to go to the camp, but I'll be back shortly.' He got off the bed. 'Try and get some sleep. We'll talk in the morning.'

Something in his words, in his face, some dark fleeting image of danger, sent a chill through her. She sat bolt upright in bed. 'Why? Why do you have to go to the camp? There's no reason. You were there this afternoon.'

He sighed heavily. 'Rana, it's no use. I have to go and you know it. And you also know why.'

Her eyes, wide with fright, stared into the depths of his. 'I don't know it. I don't know it at all. What are you going to do?'

'I have to settle things with Stewart, Rana,' he said tonelessly.

Her laughter verged on hysteria. 'That's stupid, it'll be a wasted trip—he's gone by now. He probably left hours ago.'

He sat down beside her on the bed and took her small hand in his. 'I can't let it go, girl. It has to be settled. Stewart is waiting and I have to go. Can't you see that if I did ignore what happened here tonight, if I did let him get away with it, without——'

'But he didn't get away with it, Heath. He didn't. You stopped him and you frightened him away. It's over and he'll never bother me again.'

'Rana, I know you're not used to our ways, but surely you can hear the error in what you're saying. I'm going and there's nothing you can do or say to stop me. I do what I have to do.'

She pulled her hand from his. 'Don't touch me! You're all the same, aren't you? Savage and violent. This is sick, I can't believe it's happening. First this afternoon and now ... now you're going out ... to do what? To fight him and maybe kill him ... or even get killed?'

'You're my wife, Rana.' Heath's voice hardened. 'I protect what's mine. It's that simple.'

'Oh yes, I nearly forgot. That's it, isn't it?' she said bitterly. 'I'm your property, and you protect your property, don't you?' He flinched beneath the lash of her words, but she drove on. 'I don't care what you do. Go away—go and get killed. I don't care! And you know I don't.' She threw herself down on the rumpled bed, smothering her sobs in her pillow. But I do care, she thought brokenly, I do care. I've tried not to, all these months, but it's no use.

Hours later, lying tense and awake, she heard the sound of the jeep pull up outside the house. It seemed forever before she heard Heath's weary footsteps echo across the verandah, the squeaking of the screen door, and the barest click as he held it from banging shut. She slipped back the sheets and slid out of bed, her bare feet moving silently over the cool pine floor. 'Heath?' she called quietly from the door of her room. 'Where are you? Why don't you turn on the light?'

He did not answer. Her eyes searched the darkness for sight of him. Heath?'

'Go back to bed, Rana.' His reply was a rasping whisper.

'No, I won't.' Moving suddenly across the room, she flicked on the overhead light. She gasped at the sight of him, her hands flying to her mouth in horror. He was leaning heavily against the wall, his face bruised, swollen, and bleeding; his shirt was torn and dirty, exposing a long gash across his stomach. He stared at her dully, unseeingly, and moved with painful effort into the kitchen.

'Dear God, Heath,' she whispered, 'what has he done to you?'

'No more than I did to him,' he said ruefully. 'A bit less, maybe.'

'You need a doctor. I'll call Jim right away.' She turned

towards the phone, but he reached out and took the receiver from her, decisively replacing it on the hook. 'Stop it, Rana. There'll be no doctor tonight. If you can stand the sight, help me. If not, go back to bed.'

It was useless to argue, she knew only too well the meaning of that inflexible look in his eyes and the firm thrust of his jaw; he would deal with the entire affair, from beginning to end, himself. Something within her, faced with the sight of this man to whom pride of name and honour were so important, rebelled against the things her mother had said of him. And once again the doubts and questions surfaced. How could he have done those terrible things of which her mother had accused him? Her mother was wrong—she had to be.

She looked squarely at Heath and said bluntly, 'I'll help.' She went into the kitchen to fetch the first aid kit and draw hot water, noticing that he did not question her, but accepted her offer matter-of-factly.

Afterwards, when they lay together in the quiet darkness, she spoke in a voice that was a bare whisper. 'I don't ... pretend to understand entirely, Heath, and I hated seeing what he did to you ... but I think ... I think I can accept that you did what you had to do.' It was the first time in these long months that she had given him even the slightest hint of acceptance and understanding.

He was lying close to her, his breath even and warm against her face; his bruised features looked young and intensely vulnerable. But even as she waited for his response, she realised he had already fallen asleep, and had heard nothing of what she had said. She lay for a long time listening to the rhythm of his breathing before she finally fell asleep, grasping his hand lightly in hers.

CHAPTER TEN

HAVING successfully persuaded Heath to stay in bed the next morning, Rana brought him breakfast on a tray and sat down beside him on the bed. He looked at her steadily, but said nothing.

'How do you feel?' she asked, when he had finished most of his breakfast and leaned back against his pillow.

'I've seen better days, girl,' he replied quietly, as he rubbed his forehead. 'I've got the damnedest headache.' He closed his eyes. 'Did I keep you awake last night? Was I restless?'

'No—I slept.' But she didn't tell him the truth of how little she'd slept. A few times she had been a hair's breadth away from going to the phone and calling Jim to come and have a look at him, for he had slept poorly, moaning often in his sleep. A dark, angry bruise now marked his cheek and Rana feared that he might have been hurt worse than he would let on.

He opened his eyes and looked at her. 'I'm sorry you had to go through that yesterday, Rana. Are you all right?'

'Yes, I'm fine. I think you should see Jim, though, just to be sure that nothing's broken, that ...' Seeing the worry and concern in her eyes, he reached out and gently pushed her long hair back from her face.

'I'll be okay in a few days, Rana. I've been in worse fights than this one, really.' A look of pain clouded his face. 'You'll never know how close I came to wanting to kill a man, though.' His hand gripped her hair more roughly and he pulled her to him. 'I don't know what I would have done if I hadn't come in time, if he'd hurt you ... I ...'

'But he didn't hurt me and it's over now, so let's not

talk about it any more. Please.'

'Yes,' he said, a look of reserve hardening his features. 'Yes, it's over.' Something in the tone of his voice, something in his face, sent a chill through her body. He meant more by these words and it was on the tip of her tongue to question him about it when a loud knock sounded impatiently on the screen door.

'Hello! Anybody home?' It was Jim Hinton's deep voice which boomed through the air. Rana slid out of Heath's arms and walked to the door.

'Stay where you are, Heath Markland,' she ordered. 'Now that he's here, he's going to take a look at you, no matter what you say.' She raised a warning hand to stop any arguments. 'No use letting the good doctor's talents go to waste when there's such a willing patient for him to practise on!' She grinned and walked quickly from the room.

Beth had come along as well. She and Rana sat in the shade on the verandah while Jim went in to see Heath and Rana told her briefly of the events of the evening before.

'Well then,' Beth said starchily, 'now I don't feet half as bad for Bill Stewart as I did last night.' She stiffled a giggle. 'I don't know how Heath looks this morning, but I'll tell you, Bill Stewart got hit by something akin to a fast-moving freight train when he decided to tangle with your husband. He left town this morning—for a safer, if not warmer, climate.' Beth laughed heartily, obviously used to seeing differences settled in this manner. They chatted easily for a few moments, Beth filling her in on the news from town, and making Rana laugh. Rana leaned over and touched the other woman's hand. 'I've missed you, Beth, and our talks. We must get back to the way it was.'

'I've missed you too, Rana. But I know there's been things ... problems that you and Heath had to settle ... so I waited, and I'll still wait until ...' There were tears in Beth's eyes as she looked earnestly at Rana. 'I love you both so much, you and Heath. You're the best friends I have and I want you both to be happy.' She wiped the tears from her cheeks. 'Look at me, sitting here crying like a baby! Great help I am, eh?'

Before Rana could respond, the screen door opened and Jim, followed by Heath, joined them on the verandah. Rana, concerned at seeing Heath out of bed, stood up quickly, but anything she was going to say was forestalled by Jim. 'Don't waste your breath, woman, he's the stubbornest fellow I've ever seen. You'll never keep him in that bed, so give up trying.' He waved an impatient hand at her. 'Go on, Rana, sit down.'

Somehow his gruff attitude eased Rana's fears. If Jim put up no more argument than that, then Heath was all right. She breathed a sigh of relief and watched her husband move stiffly and slowly to pull up a chair. He wore faded jeans and his unbuttoned shirt hung open, revealing a clean bandage on the cut Rana had seen across his stomach the night before. She had questioned him about it when she had first seen it, but he had refused to discuss it, or anything else about the fight, with her. It was over and it was to be forgotten.

He eased himself into the chair, his fingers awkwardly struggling with the buttons of his shirt. 'Well, well, well, if it isn't Bruiser Markland,' Beth teased. 'Out fighting at night again, are you, Heath? Going back to the wild and hairy days of your youth?' She raised an arm as if she was going to slap him on the back.

'If you touch me, Beth,' he warned, 'so help me I'll crumble at your feet. That's exactly how great I feel.'

Beth laughed unsympathetically. 'Don't worry, I'm not going to beat you up, old man.'

The conversation they shared was light and enjoyable, and Beth and Jim happily agreed to stay for lunch. But despite the levity and the good feeling of being with her friends again, Rana was aware that Heath was holding back, had erected a shield or barrier between himself and them. She wondered if Beth and Jim noticed, although they appeared not to; indeed, perhaps it was only her too fertile imagination after the emotionally charged events of the last hours. But the look of strain and reserve showed in his eyes, in the carved lines around his mouth. Maybe he was in pain. Maybe something was wrong that Jim had missed in his examination. Her thoughts were interrupted by Beth's voice.

'Would you mind if I freshened up a bit before lunch, Rana? This heat is getting to be too much for me, I'll tell you. One of these days I'm heading for the coast until I get word of rain hitting this neck of the woods.'

'Of course I don't mind. I'll start a salad and make some sandwiches.' They got up and went inside, Rana to the kitchen, Beth to the powder room. Rana quickly surveyed the choices she had available for sandwiches and walked back to ask the men what they would like, but the sound of Jim's urgent and worried voice stopped her from interrupting them.

'Damn it, man—it's me, remember? I'm your friend. We grew up together. Level with me for once, why don't you?'

'Stop it, Jim. It's my problem, not yours or Beth's. Leave it with me, I'll deal with it.'

Jim leaned forward. 'But you're not dealing with it, that's the point. What are you trying to do to yourself?' Heath shifted awkwardly in the chair as Jim continued, 'Look at you. Admit it or not, you can barely sit up. You came mighty close to the bottom line last night. Does she know what really happened? Does she?'

'No,' Heath said gratingly, 'and you're not to tell her. So lower your voice.'

'All right, but just tell me this—who in the hell do you think you are anyway? You're not God, you know. She's your wife and she deserves to know the truth. She deserves to be needed ...'

'Needed! Needed!' Heath rasped. 'Dear God, you sit there and talk to me about needing her. I need her so much, I'm nearly insane with it.'

Unable to move, Rana leaned against the wall for support.

'Why didn't you tell her the truth about last night, Heath?' Jim persisted ruthlessly.

'I didn't tell her because she didn't need to know. She's been through too much already.' His eyes blazed up at Jim. 'She's not like us, Jim. I've always known that, I guess, but I thought... Oh, to hell with what I thought. She hates what I am and how I live ... she hates it all, Jim. How do you think she'd feel if I told her what happened?'

Rana pressed her hands to her hot face, wondering desperately what the terrible thing was that Heath had not told her. Jim said heavily, 'Give her a chance, man. Just give her a chance. She's not Cheryl. She was never Cheryl.'

'I know that, I've known that from the beginning, but it still doesn't mean that we can make it together. If I don't stop things here, now, I'll end up destroying her ... and I couldn't live with that.'

'And what about you? What happens to Heath Markland in all of this?'

'Heath Markland doesn't matter, Jim. Not any more.'

Jim stood up and flung his chair angrily aside, his face livid. 'You're crazy, do you know that? Stewart damn near killed you last night. He tried to use that knife on you and you couldn't have stopped him, you were so blasted careless. If it weren't for Vic and Curtis, Rana would be burying her husband today. And she deserves to know ...' he stopped and swallowed, finding it difficult to continue, 'that the man she's married to needs her, that he's human and he's hurting, and he needs a reason to stop trying to destroy himself.'

Heath glared up at him. 'You don't make sense.'

'Oh, don't I? I wasn't there, but Vic and Curtis said you bloody well knew what kind of fighter Stewart was and you were careless. And then, Mr Almighty, when you can barely walk away from the whole thing, you don't come to me or Beth, and you don't talk to Rana about it.' Jim held his hands in a pleading gesture. 'You can't live like that, Heath. I know you—you need more. You're destroying yourself and I can't find out why. You won't talk to me and soon ... soon I'm going to wash my hands of you too, because I'm not so masochistic that I like torturing myself, even if you do.' He slapped the railing with an angry hand and lapsed into a frustrated silence.

For a long moment Rana was sure the conversation had ended, that Heath would not respond. Her heart thudded in her breast. Heath had nearly died last night and he had said nothing to her; he had been unable to share the fear and the agony with anyone. Tears filled her eyes at the thought of what she had done to him, of how she had forced him to live, so desperately alone all these months. 'There's nothing that you or Beth or anyone can do, Jim. It's over.' The last two words rang in her ears. 'It's over.' He had said the same thing this morning, in the same way.

'What do you mean? What's over?' demanded Jim.

'Rana and I ... our marriage ... it's finished. It was a mistake from the very beginning.'

'Hell, man, but you're not making any sense at all. That girl loves you and you love her. How is that "over"? Granted it's having a very stormy beginning, but I don't accept that it's over.'

Rana held her breath, silent tears wetting her cheeks. Almost ... almost she knew what Heath's next words would be. She knew suddenly that she had convinced him.

'No, you're wrong, Jim,' Heath whispered. 'She doesn't love me and she sure as hell doesn't need me. I'm no good for her ... I never was. She married me to escape her mother and the kind of life that was stealing the very heart of her. But she didn't marry me because she loved me. The truth is that she hates me and everything I stand for. And if we stay together, it'll kill her ... like it's killing me.' He looked unflinchingly at Jim. 'I love her, Jim, more than I've ever loved anyone. I thought, given time, that she'd come to love me, to understand what she means to me, but it hasn't worked out that way ... and I can't fight it any more. I'm sending her home to Edmonton at the end of the week, back to the people she belongs with. She wants a divorce and I'm going to give it to her. It *is* over, Jim.'

Rana squeezed her eyes shut against the pain of his words, and the agony in his voice. No ... no, Heath, she prayed, don't send me away. Don't make me live without you.

A slight sound made her open her eyes. Beth stood looking at her, plainly having overhead Heath's words. She reached out and took Rana's hand in hers and led her to the kitchen. 'What are you going to do, Rana?'

'You know, don't you? You know everything?'

'Yes, we both know. We've known Heath a long time, child. It would have been impossible not to.'

'I love him, Beth. I do love him.' Her throat ached and the tears wouldn't stop. The pain in her heart wouldn't cease.

'I know you do, and I know how much that man out there loves you. You both have so much to give one another, if you'd only let it happen.'

'Oh, Beth, you have no idea what I've done to him,' Rana sobbed. 'You can never guess the things ... the horrible things I've said to him, the things I've believed of him, I've hurt him so much ...'

Beth put a gentle hand on her shoulder. 'You're very young, dear child, and it isn't easy to live with another person. It takes getting used to ...'

'Oh no,' Rana said bitterly, 'it's nothing as simple as all that. I believed lies, horrible lies, about him.' She shuddered at the thought. 'My mother, she said ... she said he'd stolen, forced my father to sell out to him and that I was just something else he wanted and took because he was used to getting what he wanted. She said that Heath caused Daddy's death, that losing the business to Heath killed him. And I believed her. I didn't even trust my own husband, Beth. I loved him and I could see what kind of man he really was, but no, I believed my mother's lies. She poisoned everything and I let her. I let her do it.' She was nearly beside herself now, crying uncontrollably. Beth, frightened by the desperate look in the girl's eyes, tried to calm her.

'I'll get Jim, maybe he'll give you something to calm you down.'

But Rana reached out and held her hand, stifling her sobs with a visible effort. 'I've made his life a living hell these past six months, Beth. He deserves better than that.' She stood up and smoothed back her hair, smiling wanly. The fact that she had made a difficult decision was evident in her eyes and the firm set of her jaw. 'If he still wants me, Beth, I'll stay and be a real wife to him. But right now, I need to think, on my own. Please let me do this by myself.'

Beth nodded slowly, hoping that the girl was strong enough after everything she'd been through. 'Talk to Heath, child, work it out together.'

'Yes ... we will. We must,' Rana breathed fiercely. 'We must.'

A shout from one of the men drew their attention. 'Beth! Come here!' Jim yelled urgently.

They hastened into the living room, to see Heath struggling with his boots. He spoke quickly, with authority. 'It's happened. Vic just came by. There's an outbreak of fire south of here and it's getting larger and moving fast.' He tucked in his shirt and strode over to Rana. 'I want you to go into town and stay with Beth until I come for you. You'll be safe there.'

'No. Please,' her voice quivered, 'let me stay here. I need to stay here, Heath. I'll be safe, really I will.'

He looked at her, about to argue, then shrugged and gave in. 'All right, but leave the radio on and if there's the slightest change in wind direction and the fire starts moving this way, you get yourself into Rexton immediately. Do you understand me?'

'Yes, I understand. I'll do exactly what you say. I'll wait here for you, Heath.'

'You don't wait here for me if it shifts in this direction,' he reiterated roughly. 'It might cut you off before I could get here. I'll call you on the radio, so stay close.' He gently squeezed her slim shoulder and for a moment looked as if he would bend and kiss her, but then turned quickly and ran down the steps to his jeep, Jim and Beth following close behind.

Beth called back to her. 'You're sure you won't come with us, Rana? It'd be safer, just in case ...'

'Yes, I'm sure. I'll wait here ... for Heath,' she said evenly. She was firmly resolved to stand beside him this time, to take her place as the wife he deserved, as the wife she had refused to be for far too long.

If possible, it was hotter that day than any she could remember all summer. Huge white clouds hung heavily over the hills, the smell of smoke acrid in the still air, and the sky bearing a slight yellow tinge. Rana grew weary and restless after hours of waiting within earshot of the radio and finally wandered down to the lake. She swam for a while, but, strangely enough, did not find that the activity provided any relief. Within moments of her getting out of the water, the oppressive heat gripped her again. Gradually she became aware of a feeling of foreboding growing within her. Attributing it to the intense heat, she walked slowly back to the house. Moments later, Beth Hinton's voice sounded over the radio and Rana picked up the receiver.

'Beth? This is Rana. What's the news? Where's Heath?'

'Where have you been?' Beth sounded worried. 'Heath's been trying to get you. He finally called me, thinking that maybe you'd decided to come into town.'

'Damn! I wish I hadn't missed him. I just went down

to the lake for a swim. It's so hot I can barely move. Is Heath all right?'

'Yes, but it doesn't look good out there. They're fighting a big one this time, but not to worry, it's not heading for Clearwater ... not yet anyway. Heath wants you to come into town—he won't be able to get back there at all tonight and says you'll be safer here.'

'No, Beth. I've told you, I belong here. I want to wait here for him.'

'Don't be so foolish, Rana. You can wait here with us just as easily.' Beth hesitated, then added, 'Do you have any idea how quickly the entire situation can change? A simple shifting in wind direction, and that fire could be bearing down on you. I don't understand why he didn't force you to come into town with us.'

'Don't be ridiculous, Beth. I'm perfectly safe here.' Rana spoke more quietly now. 'It's important that I wait for him here, Beth. Please understand. I want him to know that I belong at Clearwater ... with him.'

'You're as stubborn as he is, Rana! All right, do what you have to do, but for heavens' sake, stay by the radio tonight, sleep next to it even. That's the only way you'll know if there's a wind shift or a fresh outbreak. Do you understand what I'm telling you?'

'Yes, I promise. I'll stay close. And Beth?'

'Yes?'

'Are you sure Heath's all right? I mean ... he didn't seem well enough this morning to go off to fight a forest fire.'

'Listen to who's talking! He does what he thinks he has to do, too. Now who might that remind you of? I told you you were a matching pair. All kidding aside, I'm sure he'll be okay, Rana. He knows how to take care of himself out there, he was born to it. Look, I've got to run. Call if you need anything and I'll keep you posted from this end.'

Later that evening Rana did call Beth. The other woman's voice sounded strained and concerned as she gave her an update on the fire. 'I knew this was going to happen, I just knew it. The weather's been a killer all summer, just getting ready for the big one, and this seems to be it. It's out of control and things are going to get worse, I can feel it.'

'Where's Heath?'

'I haven't heard a word from him since noon. He was on one of the fronts, so God knows if it's possible for him to get to a radio. Would it do any good if I ordered you into town right now? This thing's got me scared, Rana, and I just don't understand him letting you stay out there. Be sensible, just this once.'

'Heath will come for me soon, Beth, I know. I'm going to be fine.'

Beth's voice rose in frustration. 'Heath can't come for you, Rana, don't you understand that? I'm sure he can't get away now.'

'It's no use, Beth. I'm waiting here. I'll talk to you later.' Rana quickly replaced the receiver and walked out on to the verandah. She didn't want to be persuaded to leave.

It was dark, but the sky to the south glowed and reflected red in the blackness. The smell of burning wood permeated the air. For a moment Rana truly considered taking Beth's advice. She could pack a few things and be in town in half an hour or so. But just as quickly she dismissed the entire idea, for she could not bring herself to leave Clearwater. This was home and she belonged here with Heath. She would show him, by remaining here and waiting for him to come for her, that she had, at last come to him.

For most of the night Rana slept fitfully, the heat seeming undiminished, even after sundown. She tossed and turned and finally fell into a heavy sleep. It was nearly dawn when something indefinable awakened her. Her heart pounded as she got out of bed and walked out on to the verandah. Something was wrong. The feeling was sharper and clearer within her now. The sun had not yet risen, while a strong breeze blew from the south, strangely warm for so early in the morning. A heavy mist hung over the lake. Then it struck her. The wind had changed during the night. The mist on the lake wasn't mist at all. It was smoke.

CHAPTER ELEVEN

OVER and over again during the morning Rana tried to reach Beth, or anyone else who would answer her, on the radio. Although she could hear others talking, try as she might, the transmitter would not work. No one acknowledged her increasingly frantic calls.

She paced the living room floor, back and forth, over and over again, wishing desperately for the sound of Heath's jeep. But he did not come.

It was nearly noon when Rana finally realised she could wait no longer. In fact, she had a terrible gnawing fear that perhaps she had already waited too long—she should have left for Rexton at dawn. Now, across the lake, smoke billowed high and red-hot flames licked at the sky. She stood on the wharf watching Heath's plane bobbing desolately in the water.

It was then that she became aware that the smoke was not only drifting across the lake from the south but was also edging in from the north, from the direction of Rexton. Panic welled within her as she ran across the lawn and into the house. She fumbled in her handbag for the keys to the car, finally turning the entire contents out on the kitchen counter. She grabbed the keys, clumsily sweeping the mess she had made on to the floor. Leaving it where it fell, she rushed outside.

Out on the verandah she stopped suddenly and leaned weakly against the railing. 'Heath,' she pleaded in her mind, 'please help me. I don't know what to do, where to go.' A rising feeling of nausea seized her, then gradually receded. She knew that she had to get to Rexton—somehow. Heath would look for her there.

A bare five miles from Clearwater, however, she realised that it was no use. The road to Rexton was blocked, engulfed in flames. She could hardly see a hundred feet in front of her and the heat had become unbearable—she could go no further. She braked and put the car in reverse, manoeuvring to turn it around on the narrow road. Within minutes she was heading back to Clearwater. She should have listened to Beth, she told herself angrily, and to Heath's first warning; she should have gone into Rexton yesterday.

Suddenly the tall figure of a man emerged from the woods, stumbling and then standing erect, raising his arms and signalling her to stop. She slammed on the brakes and brought the car to a skidding halt. Through the mist of her tears she recognised him. 'Heath!' she shouted. Swinging the door open, she leapt from the car, ran the short distance that separated them, and flung herself into his embrace. His strong arms closed around her and he lifted her off the ground, holding her tightly, almost squeezing the breath from her. She felt the violent thudding of his heart against her body.

'Girl,' he moaned, 'I thought ... I thought I'd lost you ...'

'I knew you'd come for me ... I knew you would,' she stammered excitedly, her words mingled with tears of happiness at the sight of him.

As quickly as he had drawn her close, he put her down and pushed her away. Immediately she missed the security of his hold and moved back towards him. But he held her at arm's length. 'No, Rana!' Anger blazed in his eyes. 'What in God's name do you think you're about, anyway? I told you to get into Rexton if there was the slightest danger. I was a fool to trust you. I should have put you bodily into Jim and Beth's car.'

'Please, Heath ... let me explain,' she pleaded.

'I've no time for your explanations, Rana, we have to get out of here—now.'

She nodded, seeing the lines of worry and tiredness that furrowed his face; he obviously had not slept since he left yesterday morning. 'But how did you get here?' she questioned, half turning and raising a hand to indicate the road to Rexton. 'The road's impassable.'

'I know, damn it. I started out on it at dawn this morning to get you when Beth radioed me that she'd had no contact with you since last night. She's nearly beside herself with worry. It's about time you thought of someone other than yourself, don't you think?' Rana lowered her head, avoiding the look of censure in his eyes. 'The wind shifted late last night and with Clearwater directly in its path, she—and I—expected you in Rexton.'

'But Heath, the fire's south of Clearwater. How could the road to Rexton be cut off? It's impossible.'

'The impossible happens here sometimes, Rana. There's at least a half dozen more major outbreaks, and we, right now, are wedged very neatly between two of them; and they're both moving fast. I had to turn back when I couldn't get through by road.' He added impatiently, 'But let's leave all the explanations and discussion for later—if there is a later.'

Fear surged within her. 'What do you mean?'

'I mean that we have to really move if we're going to make it out of here alive. We can't go back to Clearwater—we're probably already cut off from the lake. I came through by canoe and it was close going in places even then.' He grabbed her by the wrist and pulled her after him as he leapt from the road down on to a trail that led through the woods to the river. 'I beached the canoe on the river, we'll get to it as quickly as we can and make a run for it into Rexton.'

'But Heath ...' she hesitated, 'that part of the river—there's a long stretch of white water ... can we ...'

'For God's sake, Rana, it's our only chance. You've got to trust me, there's no other way.' He stared down at her, his eyes deep and inscrutable.

'Yes—I do trust you. Let's go,' she said confidently.

He turned and quickly led the way towards the river. He began at a fast walk and soon broke into a run. At times it seemed to Rana that they were heading full into the face of the fire, but without question she followed him, her legs weak and trembling, her heart feeling as if it were about to burst. Heath ran like a man possessed, dodging now into the smoke and then turning off abruptly, running over rough terrain away from the fire. Twice she fell, and twice he came back for her, lifting her quickly to her feet and starting out again the second time firmly holding her wrist and half pulling, half dragging her after him. The air was white hot and pungent with smoke so that they coughed and choked, gasping for breath. Rana's eyes watered and her vision blurred. Again she stumbled and fell, this time pulling him down with her. Half blinded by the smoke, they lay together for a moment on the ground, panting for a slim breath of the clean air that lay under the smoke.

But respite was shortlived. Again Heath lifted her to her feet, her aching body screaming in protest. 'Come on, girl!' he yelled 'You've got to try. We won't make it if you don't.' A spasm of coughing caught him and he bent over, gasping for air.

'No, leave me,' she pleaded. 'Please—I can't go on. Save yourself, Heath.' She was crying now, her eyes stinging with the heavy smoke. She backed away from him, not seeing that she stood on the edge of a bluff, which dropped off behind her at a steep angle. A strangled cry broke from her lips when she turned her head slightly and realised her precarious position. She fought to retain her balance but would have fallen had Heath not moved quickly forward and thrust her back from the edge. However, his sudden movement at such an awkward angle caused him to lose his footing, and to her horror he plunged over the side.

Rana screamed, and watched in terror as his body

rolled to the bottom of the bluff. She heard him moan in pain as he hit a jagged rock; then he lay still. 'Heath? Heath? Are you all right?' she cried struggling down a path at the side of the bluff, half running and half sliding with the loose rock. She reached his inert body and knelt beside him. 'Heath? Speak to me ...' she reached out to him, laid a hand on his shoulder, and tried to pull him on to his back.

His body stiffened at her touch. His voice a strangled whisper, he managed to say, 'Don't touch me, Rana. Just leave me for a minute, until I figure out what's wrong.'

Slowly he struggled to his knees, his face buried in one of his arms. 'Please, Heath,' she pleaded, 'let me help you.' Again she reached out and tried to pull him to a sitting position. He gasped in pain and doubled over, his breath coming in ragged gulps. 'Heath? What did I do? What's wrong?'

It was then that she saw his left arm, lying helpless and bent at a grotesque angle beside him. 'Oh, my God, Heath—your arm ... is it broken?'

He looked up at her, his eyes glazed with pain, sweat beading his forehead. 'Get to the river, girl ... just follow the trail ... it goes straight to where I beached the canoe ... it's just ahead a short distance ... hurry ... you don't have much time.'

She looked around her, confused by his words. 'I don't understand. What about ...' Then she realised that he was telling her to go without him—to leave him and save herself. 'No! I won't leave you and you can't make me,' she yelled, defiance blazing in her eyes.

Lines of agony carved themselves in his face as he struggled to sit up. 'You've got to, Rana. There's no reason for us both to die here. You've got to save yourself.' With his good arm, he reached out and tried to push her to her feet. 'Dear God, girl, please don't do this ... don't ...'

A steel core of strength and determination hardened within her. 'I asked you if it was broken. Is it?'

'No, I don't think so. I think the shoulder's dislocated.'

'Can't you walk with it then?'

'We'd never make it.' He looked at her in frustration. 'Rana, you've got to go without me, there's no other way.'

'I won't leave you, Heath. Can we set it? Do you know what to do?'

'Okay, we'll try.' He raised himself to a kneeling position, opposite Rana. 'But if you can't set it the first time, Rana, there's no second chance. You'll have to go ahead of me to the river. I'll follow, and believe me, I'll do my best to get there, but you stand a better chance without me.' He waited for her agreement. 'Do you understand what I'm saying to you, Rana?' he demanded, desperation evident in his eyes. 'This is no game and we're wasting precious time arguing about it.'

'I'm not arguing,' she replied evenly. 'Just tell me what to do about your shoulder.'

He stared at her, then spoke. 'Bring my elbow close to my side and slightly towards my back.' She did as she was told, flinching as he drew in a sharp breath. 'Easy, girl ... be easy.'

She could tell by his pallor just how much it hurt him. In a ragged whisper he went on, 'Hold the elbow there and turn my forearm out at a right angle from my side.' He closed his eyes and did not speak for a moment, the sweat running in small rivulets down his face. 'Okay. Now just listen to me first and then do exactly what I say ... I don't think I can stand another try, and we don't have the time anyway. It'll have to work the first time or not at all.'

'I'm listening, Heath. Tell me, quickly!'

'All right. Very slowly lift my elbow upward and then bring my forearm quickly across my chest ... but keep my elbow raised.'

Rana didn't move.

'Do you understand what I said?' he questioned urgently.

'Yes—yes, I understand.'

'Then do it! Come on, Rana. For God's sake, do it!'

Bracing herself, and taking a deep, steadying breath, she did as she was told and to her unutterable relief felt the head of his arm bone slip back in place with a sharp click. Heath expelled a long breath and leaned forward, his forehead resting on her shoulder. But only moments later he pulled himself to his feet, swaying unsteadily at first, but gradually regaining his balance. He tore off his shirt and fashioned a sling for his arm, Rana helping him by tying it in a knot at his neck.

He took her hand in his and pulled her gently after him. 'Come on, girl—we're close to the bottom line.'

Somehow, by the grace of some unnamed miracle, they made it to the river. Heath helped her into the canoe and pushed off. 'We'll stay in the centre of the river, and hope for the best where it narrows.'

'But what about your arm? How can you even paddle?'

He slipped it carefully out of the sling and gripped the paddle. 'We don't have a whole lot of choice.' The white lines of pain etched around his mouth told her what this effort was costing him. 'Nor do we have a whole lot of time,' he added grimly.

They moved off down the river, making good time when the current was strong, but the effort they expended when the river deepened and the current slowed was a grinding and killing one. They were within two miles of the town when they rounded a bend in the river and Heath, looking at what lay ahead of them, expelled a weary, almost defeated breath. 'Dear lord,' he groaned, 'we can't make it through that.' He stopped paddling, and stared ahead at the fire which raged white hot on both sides of the river.

'Can we make a run for it, Heath?' Rana asked, mesmerised by the leaping orange flames.

He shook his head. 'We'd never make it. The heat's more than we could stand.'

'Then what are we going to do? Is there no way out?'

Heath looked around him. The fire burned behind them now, as well. There was no going back, and there was no going ahead. 'We stay here,' he said tonelessly. 'We stay right here. Into the river, Rana.'

She stared at him, not understanding the meaning of his words. 'What?'

'I said get out of the canoe. I'll tip it so we take cover underneath ... and pray to God that we get enough breathing time.'

Rana slipped over the side into the river, searching with her feet for the bottom, 'Heath,' she cried out, it's too deep here—we can't even stand up!'

He slid into the water next to her, putting a calming hand on her shoulder and managing a half grin. 'I know, but we can't have everything our way, now can we?'

She looked at him, openly admiring the sheer strength and will power of this man who had struggled so valiantly against such awesome odds to bring them to safety. 'Well, Heath, as Eli used to say, "some days you just can't make a nickel." I have the feeling that this might be one of those days.'

He laughed heartily, 'That's my girl!' But then he quickly grew serious and pushed her away from the canoe. 'Dive under and come up inside when I've tipped it.' She nodded her understanding of his instructions and did as she was told.

Inside, the blackness was frightening and she reached out for him, treading water desperately. His deep voice reassured her as his hand touched hers. 'Hold on to the seat, Rana, no need to tread water all the time. Breathe slowly and quietly, we'll use less air that way. We've precious little to spare.'

Minutes passed like hours; the darkness was oppressive and the heat seemed unbearable. Many times Rana felt that she could not continue to struggle, wanting only to release her grip on the canoe and slide under to a deeper and more comforting darkness. Somehow Heath seemed to sense those times and increased the pressure of his hand on hers or whispered words of comfort. 'Hold on, Rana, just a little while longer. We'll come through it . . . don't give up now, not when we're nearly there.'

'I can't . . . I can't,' she sobbed brokenly, feeling her fingers relax their hold on the canoe and the warm water move up over her chin and her face. She felt his arms draw her against the roughness of his chest and hold her fast to him.

'Yes, you can—and you will. We've come this far and we're going the rest of the way. I won't let you give up, girl . . . do you hear me?' He spoke in ragged breaths, for they were nearly out of air and he knew it. She nodded silently and then leaned her full weight against him, her body cradled against his, giving herself completely into his care and keeping.

He stirred against her. 'Rana? Can you hear me?'

'Yes . . .'

'I'm going . . . outside . . . to check. Don't let go . . . whatever you do . . . don't let go . . .'

He folded her fingers around the wooden seat and disappeared beneath the surface, returning moments later. 'I think it's okay—we may be able to make it now.'

The sight that greeted her as she rolled back into the canoe was devastating. The forest was black and charred and a pall of thick smoke hung heavily over the water. 'No . . . no . . .!' Her voice rose to an hysterical pitch. 'No . . . we can't . . .'

She was out of control now, her erratic movements unbalancing the canoe. Heath's strong hands seized her by the shoulders and shook her. 'Stop it, Rana! Stop it!' he demanded. 'We won't make it if you don't pull yourself together.'

She twisted away from him. 'Why don't you just leave me?' she screamed. 'I'm so tired . . . and I want to stay here. Go away . . . just go away. You shouldn't have come after me in the first place ... it was over ... you said so yourself. I hate you! I hate you!'

She didn't see his arm move until she felt the stinging flat of his hand against her face. Her sobbing ceased as she stared at him in wonder. Her fear receded and a strange calm filled her. She touched her cheek, her slim fingers steady now. 'Yes,' she said evenly, 'yes. We must go now.'

They slowly guided the canoe through the narrow passage in the river, and out into deeper, yet swifter water. The current helped them now, taking them closer and closer to safety—to Rexton. After a while Heath stopped paddling, calling to her to rest for a moment, as he leaned his head forward on the paddle that lay across his knees.

For the first time Rana consciously considered the cost to Heath of the brutal beating that he had taken during the past thirty-six hours, and wondered at the steel-like control and strength of him. An angry purple bruise had spread from his shoulder across the upper part of his chest and the marks from his fight with Bill Stewart had not yet faded. It was evident in his face, in the glazed look in his eyes, that every movement now meant agony for him. But still he refused to give up.

He straightened slowly and spoke to her, his voice quiet and strained. 'Rexton's only a mile and a half from here, but ... there's white water between us and it. I don't think ... I have the strength to bring us through that way. We'll have to beach the canoe and go the rest of the way on foot. I'll get us as close as I can though ...'

She nodded and followed his lead, beginning to paddle again. The current was noticeably stronger now and she did not have to work as hard. The roar of the rapids ahead filled her ears and through the trees that had escaped the ravages of the fire, she caught a welcome glimpse of Rexton nestled in the valley ahead; she was relieved that the fire had come no closer to the town.

'Oh, Heath! We made it ... we've done it, darling!' she yelled excitedly, turning abruptly in her seat to look at him. The look on his face silenced her immediately. Something was wrong—dreadfully wrong. He had stopped paddling and was gripping the side of the canoe with his right hand. His left arm hung lifelessly at his side.

'Rana ...' he breathed, shaking his head to remove the web of darkness that clouded his eyes, 'move it to shore ... hurry ... I can't ...' He lurched upright, flailing against some unseen assailant, fighting a desperate and losing battle for consciousness. His eyes closed and he plunged over the side, tipping the canoe with his sudden movement.

Rana went under and quickly resurfaced, choking on the water she'd swallowed. 'Heath!' she called frantically. She saw him struggling weakly in the water ahead of her, being drawn slowly, inexorably, downstream towards the rapids. 'Dear God, please help me,' she pleaded silently, feeling the pull of the river on her slim body as she struck out towards him. She reached him in moments, grabbed hold of his arm and struggled to bring him to shore. Her arms ached with the effort and deep within her she knew that to fight against the pull of the current was useless. But she couldn't give up—he hadn't given up on her. She had to bring him to safety, to keep him from the foaming rage of the river ahead, to save him from being dashed and broken against the jagged rocks. They had come too far, gone through too much, to have it end that way.

But the shoreline receded, and it seemed that with every stroke she took they were pulled further downstream. She fought against the water swirling about her face. Heath had regained consciousness and with the little strength he had left he twisted his body towards her and took her in his arms. 'Don't fight it, girl ... no more ... fighting ...' His words came slowly, broken by his attempt to keep his head above water. 'We can't ... get back to shore ... let it carry us down ... there's still a chance ... stay with me ... no matter what ... don't let go of me ...'

His arms held her in a vice-like grip, a grip so strong that she wondered again at his reserves of inner strength. They clung to one another, desperate and still willing to make one final effort to live.

CHAPTER TWELVE

'RANA ... Rana ...'

Hearing the sound of her name, faint and distant, she stirred, but couldn't pull back the dark cover that held her to the earth. She felt the cool wet ground beneath her and pressed her bruised body to it, refusing to leave it. However, strong hands seized her, seeking to pull her away from her new-found comfort.

'No ... no ... leave me ... just leave me ...' she muttered, her eyes still closed.

'Not yet, girl ... you need a doctor ... we have ... to keep going ...'

Slowly she opened her eyes. It was dusk, but looming above her she could make out Heath's taut features. 'Heath?' she said shakily, gently touching his bruised cut face. Suddenly aware of the stillness surrounding them, she knew with a certainty that they were at last safe. They'd made it. 'Oh, Heath, thank God! We've come through after all!'

But she saw no relief in Heath's eyes, in the tense line of his shoulders. 'Rana, we have to get to Jim's.' He reached out and drew her into his arms, but the lifting movement, however careful, sent a searing wave of pain through her body. She stiffened, trying to fight it, frantically grabbing at his neck.

'Heath!' The long shrill scream filled the silent darkness until it was no longer a part of her, but outside of her, fading and passing away into nothingness.

'Jim ... Beth ... help me ...'

During the long walk from the river into Rexton, Rana recovered consciousness continually aware of the burning pain within her, and of the man who carried her. She clung to him, begging him to stop the ravages of the agony that assaulted her. And now he stood in the road outside Jim and Beth's unable to move any further, fighting to retain his tenuous hold on reality. His voice barely audible, he called out again.

She heard the screen door open and light flooded out on to the road. A man emerged. 'Who's there?' Jim's deep voice questioned, as he kicked the door shut behind him.

'Jim ... please ... I need ...' Jim's stocky figure swam before Heath's eyes, the roaring in his head submerging him, making him lose his hold on the slim body he held in his arms. 'Take her, Jim ... she's hurt ... badly ... lost a lot of blood ...'

Jim covered the distance between them in seconds, calling to Beth over his shoulder as he ran. He took Rana from his friend, as Heath sank slowly to his knees in the dust.

Rana's eyes flickered, opened for a moment, then closed. Clean shafts of yellow sunlight cut through the dimness of the hospital room. She moved slightly, tentatively, not wanting to resurrect the pain that she had endured last night. A soft sigh escaped her as she became aware of the cool sheets upon which she lay, and she sank back into the peaceful darkness that surrounded her with safety and security. Images, blurred and fleeting, floated through her mind. Heath had come for her, as she knew he would. They were together at Clearwater. Dawn. The trees, green velvet in a startling depth of blue. The sweet smell of rain carried on a soft summer wind. Heath—her husband, her love, strong, proud, and indomitable—standing by the lake. Waiting. A silhouette alone against the sky.

She whispered his name, softly calling him to her. 'Heath?'

A hand, cold and thin, touched her face, banishing her gentle thoughts with a suddenness that frightened her. 'Heath?' she called again, willing him to come to her.

'Hush, child, everything's all right now. You're safe.' A voice, as thin and cold as the hand that still lay on her cheek, crooned in the darkness. 'Mother's here now. He'll never hurt you again.'

The girl's eyes flew open. Her mother, Dorothea Liscombe, sat by her bed. In silence Rana tried to comprehend where she was—it looked like a hospital room. What had happened? She turned her head to look more closely at the woman who sat rigidly beside her. 'Mother?'

'Yes, child, I'm here. Everything's fine, just relax. I'll take care of everything, just as I always did.'

'I . . . don't understand. What's happened?'

A look of shock crossed Dorothea's tightly controlled features. 'Oh, my poor baby. Don't think about it now. It's probably just as well that you don't remember anything . . . at least not until you're stronger.'

Undisguised fear filled Rana at the implication of these words. Something dreadful had happened and she couldn't remember what. Heath? Where was Heath? She wanted him now, needed him, and the strength and reassurance of his presence.

'Where's Heath? I want him . . .'

'He's gone.' Two words, clipped and cutting. A pronouncement, the nature of which Rana did not comprehend.

The heavy door swung open and Jim Hinton, followed by a silent and obviously concerned Eli, entered. Eli walked across the room, bent down and kissed her cheek. 'Hello, dear. It's good to see you awake. You scared the living daylights out of me. You know that?'

She gripped his strong, weathered hand. 'Eli—something's wrong and Mother won't tell me what it is. She says it's better that I don't remember. I don't know where Heath is ... she says he's gone ... I can't remember ...' She rubbed her forehead, as if to force the memories back, tears streaming down her pale face.

Eli straightened, anger evident in his eyes. 'Damn it, Dorothea! I think you've done just about enough to this child. What in hell have you said to her?'

Dorothea sat straight in the chair, her hands clasped tightly. 'And I've had just about enough of you this morning, Eli Liscombe! Rana is my child, do you understand me? And I'll do what I think is right to protect her and you will kindly stay out of it.'

The old man moved threateningly around the bed. 'No, I won't. I've stayed out of this matter for entirely too long.' He motioned to Rana. 'She's not a child, Dorothea—she's a woman. And whether you like it or not she's Heath Markland's wife.'

Dorothea stood up, walked stiffly to the window and threw open the curtains. 'That's in the past now and the sooner we forget it the better it will be for all of us. It was a most unfortunate mistake from the very beginning. I never want to hear his name again. He's gone ... and believe me,' her voice dripped hatred, 'he's best forgotten.'

'Oh God ... no ...' Rana's voice broke and stinging tears filled her eyes as the memory of their mad and desperate flight from the fire, and their final struggle with the white waters of the river, suddenly engulfed her. She fell back to the pillow. 'Heath is ... dead ... isn't he?' The wild and terrible pain in her eyes went unnoticed by Dorothea who remained, unmoved, staring out the window.

'It would be so much simpler if that were so,' she answered coldly.

'That's enough, Dorothea!' Eli said sharply, as he took her roughly by the arm. 'Get your things together.

You're coming back to Edmonton with me now. You've finished interfering in their lives, you've hurt them both enough.'

'Then ... he's not ... dead,' Rana whispered thankfully. 'Where is he, then? He's hurt—that's it, isn't it?' She looked pleadingly at Jim, who walked over to her and took her small hand in his.

'What do you say we have a little talk together, just the two of us, Rana?' He looked at Eli, who understood immediately and ushered Dorothea forcibly to the door.

'I'll be back to see you, child, before your mother and I leave for Edmonton,' he said softly as he closed the door behind them.

Jim pulled a chair close to the bed, still holding Rana's hand in his. 'You'd best get yourself back on your feet soon, Rana Markland. My Beth is driving me crazy, coming over here every day trying to see you.'

'Every day?' she questioned, puzzled.

'Yes. This is the fifth day you've been with us here at the clinic, Rana.'

She shook her head, unable to grasp the significance of what he had said. 'That's impossible, Jim. Yesterday, Heath and I, we ...'

'No, Rana, it wasn't yesterday at all. It was five days ago that Heath brought you to our place. You'd both ...' He lowered his head, the words coming with some difficulty. 'You both narrowly escaped the fire. You were badly hurt.'

Her eyes clouded with the memory of that night. 'Yes, I remember ... the pain ... But where's Heath, Jim? Why hasn't he come to see me?'

'Rana, he's been with you night and day—like a man possessed. Even when he needed sleep desperately he wouldn't leave you. But when he knew you were going to make it, he ...'

'Yes?' she asked anxiously.

'He left.'

'Left? Where did he go? Why did he leave me after

everything that happened? After all we'd been through? Why would he leave?'

Jim drew a long breath. 'For a number of reasons.' He waved a weary hand. 'There's just no easy way to say this. He had me contact your mother shortly after he brought you in and she arrived the next day. You were still unconscious and we ... we didn't know if we were going to be able to save you.'

Rana looked at him sadly. 'Mother blamed him, didn't she?'

'Yes. She didn't leave him much to go on after what had happened to you ... after you ...' he closed his eyes against his mental picture of the accusations Rana's mother had flung so brutally and callously at Heath, '... after you lost the baby.'

Stunned and immobilised by his words, she stared unseeingly into his face. 'The baby? I ... I was pregnant?'

'Yes.'

She clutched his hand, her eyes dark with a sorrow too vast for tears. 'I lost his child,' she repeated blankly. 'And my mother blamed him. After all that he did to save me ... she blamed him?' Then she crumpled in his arms, weeping uncontrollably. 'How much more can we take, Jim? This is all so senseless.'

'For the life of me, Rana, I can't see a reason for it,' he replied wearily. 'Heath and I grew up together—he's my best friend, in every sense of the word. And I can't help him. I grieve for the man who walked out of here yesterday. He blames himself for keeping you with him when you wanted a divorce, for letting you stay at Clearwater with the threat of fire so imminent, for what you had to go through trying to escape the fire, and ... for the loss of your child. Your mother didn't say anything to him that he didn't already believe.'

'Oh, Jim ...' she breathed sorrowfully. 'What must he be going through?'

'I know, I know. And I'm not sure that he can make it ... without you.'

She squared her shoulders and squeezed his hand. 'He doesn't have to make it—without me, Jim,' she replied evenly. 'I'm not leaving him. I love him . . . he must know that.'

Jim shook his head sadly. 'No, he doesn't know that. He thinks you hate him, Rana . . . and that you blame him for your father's death and everything else that's happened. He told me to tell you that you could have your freedom and whatever else you wanted as a settlement. He won't fight you.'

'Where is he?' she asked quietly.

'Back at Clearwater . . . but I don't know for how long. I think he was planning to close it up and move on.'

'He'd never do that, Jim. There's no place he loves more than Clearwater. There's nowhere——'

'That's right . . . there's nowhere for him now . . . now that he thinks he's lost you.'

The drive to Clearwater was an eternity long for Rana. It was a grey day, with a faint touch of autumn in the air. She sat, small and silent, next to Eli in the car, watching with saddened eyes the destruction wrought by the fire. Her heart ached at the sight of the black and charred forests that had, only days before, been green and alive. 'Oh, Eli . . . will it ever be the same again?'

'It'll take a long time, but it'll grow back. Not the same, but it'll grow.'

A slight tremor of fear filled her voice. 'Do you think he's still here, Eli?'

The old man looked sadly down at her. 'I don't know, child, but I hope so, I truly do.'

'Thank you, Eli.' She leaned her silken head against his shoulder. 'I only hope we can work things out.'

There was the ghost of an old anger in his voice. 'It's mostly because of your mother that you've ended up in such a mess. What she told you about Heath's father was nothing but lies. Had I known about those papers she showed you—and Richard's diary. Despite anything she said, Heath was never named in the diary. Any pressures that were upon your father came from Dorothea and always have. She has a lot to answer for.'

'I know that, Eli. If only I'd trusted Heath in the first place!'

As they rounded the bend, the sun broke through the clouds and the lake shimmered gold in the filtered light. 'There, Eli—how's that for a good omen?'

Somehow, by some miracle, the fire had passed within a half mile of their home, leaving it unscarred in the blackened landscape. Rana put a thin hand on his arm. 'He's here . . . he's still here. There's the jeep.' She pointed to it parked down on the wharf. 'Please stop here. I want to walk down . . . by myself.'

'I'll wait for you here,' he replied. But she shook her head.

'No, I want you to go back to town. I'm going . . . to be staying.'

'But . . .'

'No buts, Eli. Please!'

She kissed him tenderly on the cheek and slipped out of the car. He waited for a moment, before driving away, watching her move with a new kind of sureness and determination down the hill towards the lake. She had changed, grown up in the past months, and was now a woman who loved with maturity and strength. He prayed fervently that these two people, whom he cared for most in the world, would find peace and love together. Then he drove slowly away, leaving them to find their own destiny.

Rana stood for a while by the side of the house, searching for some sign of Heath, before moving quietly up the steps on to the verandah. Her stomach tightened with a twinge of fear at the thought of facing him again, remembering all that he had gone through in the past days and weeks, so much of it inflicted by her. She opened the screen door, its familiar squeak echoing in the silence, and walked inside.

'Who's there?' Heath's deep, resonant voice called from the kitchen. Rana did not answer but walked softly across the room and into the kitchen where he stood by the sink, drying his hands.

She was shocked by how thin and tired he looked; the last few days had taken their toll. For a moment he was frozen to utter stillness. Then he asked coldly, 'What do you want? Why have you come here?'

'I've come home, Heath.'

He turned abruptly and threw the towel on to the counter. 'This is not your home, Rana. You shouldn't have come.'

'That's ridiculous ... we have to talk. There are things we need to resolve.'

'Everything's resolved, girl,' he said unemotionally, 'everything.'

'Heath, please listen to me!'

'No. There's nothing more to be said between us. I'm sure Jim has told you that I won't fight any of your demands in the divorce. You can have whatever you want. We've nothing else to discuss—so I think you'd better leave.'

Persistently she followed him as he pushed past her to the front door and kicked it open. 'Now get out, Rana. Finished is finished.'

The hardness in his voice and the absence of any emotion made her falter. 'Heath,' she stammered, all of a sudden unsure of herself, 'I know ... I know that I've hurt you terribly. Can't you ... find it within yourself to forgive me? I——'

He interrupted her. 'There's nothing for me to forgive, Rana. You reacted quite naturally to the entire situation, as any girl with foolish romantic notions would. We didn't marry for love.' His voice roughened. 'Your mother was right—I took you because I wanted you. It was all part of the package, the takeover of the Liscombe properties. Now I'm finished with you—so you can go. You shouldn't be surprised. It must be very obvious to you by now the kind of man you married.'

'No . . .' she stammered. 'No . . . please don't say these things.' She put desperate hands to her ears to block out the sound of his ruthless words. 'I heard you when you spoke to Jim . . . I heard you tell him you loved me. I know the truth.'

Heath whirled on her. 'The truth! What truth? There is no truth, Rana. What are you trying to do to me?' He raked his fingers through his hair. 'Dear God, why did you have to come back?' Closing his eyes tightly, he leaned his head against the railing post. 'Can't you see? Can't you understand what I'm saying? I love you, but I . . . can't stay with you . . . not after everything I've done . . . everything I've destroyed.' He paused, the agony of what he was doing almost too much for him to bear. 'You have to leave me, girl.' He turned from her, his broad shoulders bent with the weight of his terrible burden. 'I'm no good for you . . . no good.'

'Heath, listen to me and then . . . then if you . . . if you want me to go, I will. You married a child, a young girl who did have her head filled with romantic nonsense, and who wasn't mature enough to trust the man she loved, and who loved her. I was wrong, so terribly wrong to believe the lies my mother told me. And afterwards, when I'd come to know with a certainty beyond words that you could never have done any of those things, I still . . . I still couldn't tell you that I believed in you and loved you. Yes, I've always loved you, Heath . . . always.' Her voice broke. 'I wanted your child more than anything in the world, Heath, but I couldn't even give you that. I wouldn't listen when you tried to talk to me about it and then . . . then . . . on the river . . . I lost . . .' Tears streamed down her pale, drawn face. 'Neither of us were to blame. We fought to survive, and the child . . . just wasn't to be. Not yet. But we could have a child, Heath. We could.' She held out her slim fingers in a poignant gesture.

'Please, Heath, don't send me away ... don't make me live without you. I couldn't ... I know I couldn't ...'

He turned to look at her, tears glistening in his own eyes. Then he stood up and held out his arms to her. 'Come here, girl.' He drew her close, his heart thudding against her face. 'I love you,' he breathed fiercely. 'You're the breath I draw, the white fire that burns and keeps me alive.' He managed a wry grin. 'You'll never escape me now, Rana. You've had your last chance.'

'Not that I shall ever want to,' she whispered, moving closer to him. 'Not that I shall ever want to, my love.'

What the press says about Harlequin romance fiction...

"...wholesome fiction...always with an upbeat, happy ending."

—*San Francisco Chronicle*

"...a work of art."

—*The Globe & Mail*, Toronto

"Nothing quite like it has happened since *Gone With the Wind*..."

—*Los Angeles Times*

"...among the top ten..."

—*International Herald-Tribune*, Paris

"The most popular reading matter of American women today."

—*The Detroit News*

"Women have come to trust these stories about contemporary people, set in exciting foreign places."

—*Best Sellers*, New York

"Harlequin novels have a vast and loyal readership."

—*Toronto Star*

Choose from this list of Harlequin Romance editions.*

422 Then Come Kiss Me
Mary Burchell
434 Dear Doctor Everett
Jean S. MacLeod
459 Second Love (Ring for the Nurse)
Marjorie Moore
481 Bachelor of Medicine
Alex Stuart
492 Follow a Dream (Hospital Pro)
Marjorie Moore
508 Senior Surgeon
Marjorie Moore
509 A Year to Remember (Nurse Secretary)
Marjorie Moore
517 Journey in the Sun (Doctors Together)
Jean S. MacLeod
535 Under the Red Cross
Juliet Shore
559 The Time of Enchantment (Nurse Wayne in the Tropics)
Anne Vinton
583 This Merry Bond
Sara Seale
634 Love without Wings (Surgeon's Wife)
Margaret Malcolm
636 The Home at Hawk's Nest (Nurse Candida)
Caroline Trench
673 Gateway to Happiness (Village Clinic)
Ann Cameron
683 Desire for the Star (Doctor's Desire)
Averil Ives
684 Doctor on Horseback
Alex Stuart
713 Harvest of the Heart (Nurse of My Heart)
Jill Christian
714 Conduct Unbecoming (Young Nurse Payne)
Valerie K. Nelson
729 One with the Wind (Surgeons at Arms)
Mary Hunton
737 Maiden Flight
Betty Beaty
746 Loyal in All (Nurse Marika, Loyal in All)
Mary Burchell
748 The Valley of Palms
Jean S. MacLeod
798 If This Is Love
Anne Weale
799 Love Is for Ever
Barbara Rowan
810 The Piper of Laide (Doctor of Rhua)
Alex Stuart
815 Young Tracy
Rosalind Brett
838 Dear Dragon
Sara Seale
872 Haven of the Heart
Averil Ives
878 The Dangerous Kind of Love (This Kind of Love)
Kathryn Blair
888 Heart of a Rose
Rachel Lindsay
902 Mountain of Dreams
Barbara Rowen
903 So Loved and So Far
Elizabeth Hoy
909 Desert Doorway
Pamela Kent
920 The Man at Mulera
Kathryn Blair
927 The Scars Shall Fade
Nerina Hilliard
941 Mayenga Farm
Kathryn Blair

*Some of these book were originally published under different titles.